# THE WHIP

"Damn!" Blade fumed, and burst from the stairwell, activating the whip. He plunged into the mass of troopers, swinging the whip like a madman, cracking it left and right, sparks flying as the whip crackled and sizzled.

Bedlam ensued. Crammed close together, the troopers were unable to fan out, unable to avoid the terrible whip. Some of them screeched as their bodies were jolted by a blow from the lash. Others endeavored to bring their batons into action, without success.

Blade whirled in one direction, then another, his right arm constantly in motion, knowing he couldn't afford to slacken his pace for an instant. The muscles in his right arm bulged as he flicked the whip every which way. He slashed a trooper's neck open and sent the trooper hurtling into those nearby. To the left he seared a trooper's eyes. The trooper was flung backwards, plowing into others, upending them in a tangle of limbs. . . .

Also in the *Endworld* series:

# DAVID ROBBINS

**ENDWORLD**

# HOUSTON RUN

LEISURE BOOKS  NEW YORK CITY

A LEISURE BOOK

Published by

Dorchester Publishing Co., Inc.
6 East 39th Street
New York, New York 10016

Printed in the United States of America

Dedicated to . . .
Judy and Joshua and ?
And
the thousands upon thousands of *Endworld* readers.
This one's for you.
Especially . . .
Brian Jones,
Joseph J. Sirak, Jr.,
Kathy Gomoll,
for your patience.
Oh.
For those who like to read between the lines—
you're in for a treat!
Enjoy!

# 1

A bright red pinpoint of light appeared in the center of the Clarke Model 2001 Computer, the navigational console for the Klinecraft Hoverjet.

"One hundred miles and closing," AS-1 announced. He occupied the middle seat in front of the control console, his seven-foot frame erect in his chair, his blue orbs scanning the digital display above the red light.

"Ready for target identification and isolation," IM-97 declared from his cushioned green seat to the right of AS-1.

In the contoured chair to the left, OV-3 flicked a silver toggle switch on the large console and a square screen before him brightened. His right hand moved across a bank of typing keys below the seven-inch-wide screen, his fingers stabbing individual letters with astonishing rapidity.

"ACTIVATED" flashed onto the screen in black block letters.

OV-3 typed his request into the computer. As a last-minute addition to the retrieval crew, he wanted to review the target data once again.

"SUBJECT: BLADE," the Clarke responded at the top of the screen, and immediately the display filled with the subject's background and peripheral data. OV-3 scanned the material.

Blade is the current head of the Warriors, the elite combat unit responsible for the security of the Home and the preservation of the Family. (Correlation: see Family & Home.) He is believed to be responsible for terminating the Doktor. Intelligence also indicates Blade terminated

Samuel II. Recent activites include confrontations with the
Technics in Chicago, and with the Soviets in Philadelphia.
This subject is considered to be extremely dangerous.

While all of the Warriors are known to be skilled
fighters, many have specialized in certain weapons. Blade is
an expert with knives, particularly the large type referred to
as the Bowie knife. He invariably carries two such knives,
in addition to whatever other arms he might require for
missions outside the Home. Intelligence has confirmed his
use of a Commando Arms Carbine on several occasions.

Physical Characteristics: Intelligence has not acquired a
photograph, and the following is based on personal des-
criptions. Height: approaching seven feet. Weight:
estimated between 220-260. Build: exceptionally strong
biological organism. Described as "all muscle from head to
toe" by one witness. Hair: dark. Worn medium length.
Eyes: gray. Distinguishing marks: none known. Marital
status: married to Family member named Jenny. One son,
Gabriel. END OF REPORT.

OV-3 pursed his thin lips. The file on Blade was unusually thin.
His hands raced over the keys, accessing the correlative material.

SUBJECT: FAMILY.

The Family resides in a walled compound in north-
western Minnesota. (Correlation: see Home.) Androxia has
not established diplomatic relations with the Family.
Evolutionary Scale Rating; 4. Industry: none. The Family's
economy is broadly communal. Stewardship is vested in the
oldest members, designated as Elders. These Elders are
responsible for the Family's educational system and for
formulating formal Family policy. One Family member is
chosen as Leader of the entire Family. Exact Family
membership is unknown, but Intelligence believes that it is
less than one hundred. Children are reared in close-knit
family units. The Family is socially primitive and scientifi-
cally ignorant.

History: Little is known. Most members are believed to
be the descendents of a survivalist group.

Disposition: Primator has decreed their eventual

subjugation and assimilation into the genetically controlled
work pool once Androxia has assumed ascendancy. Recti-
fication will be necessary. The Family is known to believe in
the fallacious concept of "love," and actively promotes
belief in a non-existent "Spirit" source and sustainer. END
OF REPORT.

OV-3 read the last section twice. Such degenerates deserved to
be exterminated. Why would Primator deal so mercifully with
these biological organisms? The genetics might be useful for
menial functions, but otherwise they were hopeless. He stared at
the monitor. The information on the Family as a whole, like that
on Blade, was singularly sparse. He decided to punch up the
report on the Home, and promptly did so.

SUBJECT: THE HOME.
The Home is a thirty-acre walled compound in north-
western Minnesota, near Lake Bronson State Park. Exact
date of construction is unknown, but it is believed to have
been built over one hundred years ago, just prior to the out-
break of World War III. The compound is surrounded by
20-foot-high brick walls. An interior moat provides additional protection from potentially hostile forces. Entrance is
afforded by a drawbridge situated in the middle of the west
wall. The eastern half of the compound is maintained in a
natural state or utilized for agricultural purposes. The
western half is devoted to socialization. Intelligence has
not mapped the interior.
The Home is defended by 12 to 15 (estimates vary)
Warriors. These Warriors are highly trained professionals.
They are divided into Triads. Known Triads: Alpha, Beta,
Gamma, and Omega. There may be more. Known
Warriors: Blade, Hickok, Geronimo, and Yama. (Correla-
tion: see individual Warriors.)
Disposition: Primator has decreed destruction after sub-
jugation of occupants. Prominence Rating: 0. END OF
REPORT.

OV-3 glanced at AS—1. "Intelligence has not compiled an
adequate file on our target," he stated.

AS-1, his attention on the 2001 console, nodded. "Did you view the data on the Home?" he asked.

"Affirmative," OV-3 replied.

"And did you note the Prominence Rating?" AS-1 inquired.

"A zero," OV-3 noted.

"Which explains our lack of information," AS-1 said. "The Family is so low on the list, they were deemed inconsequential Intelligence has been concentrating on the primaries, on the Technics, the Soviets, and the Civilized Zone."

"I understand that," OV-3 commented. "I do not understand why we are expending precious fuel to fly to a small, incon-sequential outpost merely to retrieve one organism."

"Primator wants this organism," AS-1 mentioned.

"Did Primator elaborate on his rationale?" OV-3 asked.

"No," AS-1 responded.

"I can supply a secondary reason," IM-97 chimed in.

"What is it?" OV-3 questioned.

"Clarissa," IM-97 revealed.

OV-3 gazed out the canopy of the Klinecraft Hoverjet at the stars in the night sky. "Most odd," he remarked. "What does Clarissa want with this organism?"

AS-1 shook his head. "I was not told."

"Nor was I," IM-97 said. "But I do know Clarissa petitioned Primator for the organism, and Primator assented."

AS-1 leaned over the console. "Initiate target identification and isolation," he ordered.

"Engaged," IM-97 said, and pressed a white button near his right hand. A small screen, laced with an overlaid grid, hummed and glowed with a diffuse pink light.

AS-1 studied the digital display above the red light. "Ten miles to target," he informed the others.

"What if this Blade resists?" OV-3 inquired.

"We take him alive," AS-1 said. "Primator was specific in his instructions. Any harm to the organism will result in dismantle-ment."

"And if the other Warriors interfere?" OV-3 probed.

"Any intervention is to be summarily negated," AS-1 stated.

"Understood," OV-3 said.

"Commencing deceleration," AS-1 declared.

The Klinecraft Hoverjet slowed to a mere fraction of its

cruising speed.

"Two miles to target," AS-1 told them.

OV-3 reached over and depressed a brown lever. "External lights extinguished."

"Activating Stealth Mode," AS-1 stated, and punched a black button. In the Stealth Mode, the Hoverjet's engine operated with a muted whine detectable for a range of only 25 yards.

IM-97 peered at the illuminated grid. The Burroughs Infra-Sensor Module, an optional attachment on the 2001 Computer, required several minutes to attain peak functional capability. He rested his hands on a pair of knobs below the grid, waiting for the word from AS-1.

The Hoverjet continued to wing slowly toward their destination. A minute passed in relative silence. Two minutes.

AS-1, his eyes locked on the digital display, nodded. "We are over the south wall."

"Infrared operational," IM-97 said, twisting the knob in his left hand. Dozens of red blips materialized on the grid. "Multiple possibles within range."

"Adjust the sensors," AS-1 directed. "Scan for physical dimensions, respiratory rate, and gross bulk. Our target is one of the few humans our size. He should literally stand out head and shoulders above the rest."

"Scanning," IM-97 responded.

With AS-1 handling the maneuvering of the Klinecraft, and IM-97 immersed in isolating their target, OV-3 was left with nothing to do. He elected to maximize his time by learning additional details concerning the Family. His fingers flew over the keys, and a moment later the name of another known Warrior appeared on the screen.

SUBJECT: HICKOK.

Hickok is another Warrior in the Family. (Correlation: see Home & Family.) Hickok and two other Warriors, Blade and Geronimo, are believed to constitute one of the Triads comprising the Warrior class. The name of their Triad has not been ascertained.

Hickok is known to specialize in the use of Colt Python revolvers. He is an expert marksman with handguns and rifles. Considered extremely dangerous.

Little else is known about this organism. His marital status is unknown, although one unconfirmed report claims he is married to a Warrior woman named Sherry and has one young son. Height: about six feet. Weight: estimated at 180-190. Build: lean. Hair: blond. Worn long. Also has a blond mustache. Eyes: blue. Distinguishing marks: none known. END OF REPORT.

OV-3 looked at AS-1. "I trust Intelligence will upgrade the files on the Family in the near future."

"If Primator so wills," AS-1 answered. "Evidently, the Doktor had accumulated an extensive file on the Family and the Warriors, but it was destroyed when his headquarters was obliterated. Samuel II also kept a complete dossier on them, but our spy has not been able to locate it. After Samuel II's death, his successor, the new President of the Civilized Zone, confiscated all of Samuel II's files. This President Toland allows only trusted subordinates to view the files."

"Where did Intelligence acquire our information?" OV-3 asked.

"Here and there," AS-1 replied. "Clarissa provided much of it from her memory. Some of it was obtained from monitored Soviet and Technic broadcasts. The rest came from miscellaneous minor sources. Our data on the Family is far from complete."

"That's an understatement," OV-3 commented.

IM-97 suddenly interrupted. "We have him," he declared.

"You have isolated the target?" AS-1 inquired.

"Affirmative," IM-97 affirmed. "And he has unwittingly made our retrieval easier."

"Explain," AS-1 said.

"The Infra-Sensor reveals the majority of the Family is congregated in the western section of their Home," IM-97 elaborated. "But two individuals are in the southeast quadrant. One of them must be our target. He measures out at seven feet tall and weighs 240."

"There are just two of them?" AS-1 asked.

"Just two," IM-97 confirmed.

AS-1 stared at the digital display. The Hoverjet was hovering 200 yards above the surface. He angled the Klinecraft in the direction of the pair in the southeast quadrant. "Parabolic," he ordered.

OV-3 straightened, switching a toggle to his left and gripping a round lever in his right hand. "Parabolic activated."

The Hoverjet drifted toward the southeast quadrant.

Sounds began emanating from a four-inch speaker mounted on the console near OV-3. Leaves rustling. The wind whispering.

OV-3 slowly moved the round lever back and forth, up and down, searching.

" . . . be a piece of cake," a male voice abruptly filled the cockpit.

"You think so?" responded a lower, more resonant speaker.

"I may have them," OV-3 said.

"They are the only ones in that area," IM-97 averred. "It must be them."

"I've whipped your butt two times so far, pard," the first voice stated.

"We'll try one more time," the speaker with the low tone remarked.

"Then can we call it quits for the night?" asked the first man. "I promised my missus I'd be home to tuck Ringo in. That young'un will be traumatized if his fearless papa ain't there to kiss him nighty-night."

The man with the low voice chuckled. "Sure, Hickok. This will be our last one for tonight."

"Thanks, Blade," Hickok said.

"We have him," AS-1 remarked.

"Do we take him now?" OV-3 queried.

"We will wait for a better opportunity," AS-1 said. "We do not want to arouse any suspicions. We might be able to take him when he's alone."

" . . . don't see why the blazes we have to do this anyway!" Hickok was saying.

"Practice makes perfect," Blade responded.

"After all we've been through," Hickok muttered, "we still got to play these games!"

"They're not games, and you know it," Blade corrected him. "These night drills are essential to our readiness."

"Okay. I get your drift. And I don't need no lecture," Hickok said. "Let's get this blamed nonsense over with, so we can mosey on back, tuck in the young'uns, and rustle up some grub.''

"I'll be the stalker this time," Blade said.

"Fine by me," Hickok replied.

"Mosey? Grub?" AS-1 repeated, puzzled. "This Hickok employs a peculiar dialect."

"All biological organisms are strange," OV-3 asserted.

"Blade is moving away from Hickok," IM-97 disclosed, his eyes glued to the grid.

"What are they doing?" OV-3 asked.

"Whatever it is," AS-1 speculated, "it has something to do with their Warrior training."

"I have a strange reading here," IM-97 announced, his interest piqued by a trio of bluish-red blips on the grid.

"What sort of reading?" AS-1 demanded.

"I'm picking up all of the Family members within range," IM-97 replied. "As expected, they all register red."

"All bipedal humanoids register red," AS-1 remarked.

"True," IM-97 conceded. "But I'm also registering three bluish-red life readings, about one hundred yards to the northwest."

AS-1 glanced at IM-97. "Bluish-red?"

"See for yourself," IM-97 said, waving his right hand toward the blips.

AS-1 bent to the right and peered at the grid. "But blue is for organisms lower than human, for the animal life, the mammals and reptiles and such."

"I know," IM-97 agreed. "Which is what makes these three so strange."

"They appear to be stationary," AS-1 observed.

"They are," IM-97 confirmed.

"Pulse rate?" AS-1 inquired.

IM-97 turned the right-hand knob below the grid, then studied the small figures appearing at the bottom of the screen. "Definitely not human."

AS-1 reflected for a moment. "The Burroughs unit must be malfunctioning. We know the Family maintains this half of their Home in a natural state. Perhaps the unit has detected several horses or deer and is registering a composite signal. You know how precise the calibration must be on these units. Did you calibrate it yourself?"

"No," IM-97 answered. "The craft was serviced by the technicians before our departure."

"They may have miscalibrated," AS-1 stated. "Concentrate on Blade and Hickok. We must monitor them and wait for Hickok to leave, or for them to separate."

"And then we pounce?" OV-3 interjected.

"And then we pounce," AS-1 affirmed.

# 2

Blade circled to the west, his black leather vest and green fatigue pants blending into the inky vegetation. His Bowies snuggled in their sheaths, one on each broad hip. The night air was cool, and there was a faint breeze from the west. His massive muscles rippled as he skirted a tree and reached a low rise. He crouched, grinning. The longer he took, the more irritated Hickok would become, and he needed an edge if he was to beat the gunman the third time around. The exercise was simple, yet markedly effective. One of the Warriors, in this case Hickok, acted as if he was on guard duty, standing or strolling in the open, alert for any attack. Blade's task was to sneak up on the gunfighter undetected. If he succeeded, he won. If Hickok heard him or spotted him, the gunman would win. Seemingly childish, the maneuver served to sharpen their senses. It was one of many exercises designed to keep all of the Warriors at peak effeciency. In addition to comprehensive weaponry training and advanced instruction in the martial arts, every Warrior was required to cultivate skill in the use of stealth and night combat.

The sky was a panorama of celestial lights.

Blade idly glanced up, marveling at the heavenly vista, at the magnitude of creation. He was thankful the night was moonless. It was hard enough to catch the gunman unawares as it was. A large dark cloud was floating far overhead, blotting out a cluster of stars.

Someone began whistling.

Blade flattened. He could hear someone clumping through the woods toward him. Three guesses who it was. But why, he asked himself, was Hickok making so much noise? It sounded as if the gunman was deliberately stepping on every twig and brushing against every bush in his path! What was Hickok up to now? Was the gunfighter so eager to get back to his cabin, he was intentionally making it easy for Blade to win? Or was there an ulterior motive? Blade chuckled. You could never tell with Hickok. And Blade wouldn't have it any other way. Hickok's unpredictability was a valuable asset, contributing to his sterling record as a Warrior, and had saved his life and benefited the Family in many a critical situation.

Hickok was slowly ambling to the northwest, whistling "Home on the Range."

Blade crawled behind a log, then cautiously raised his eyes above the top.

Hickok was 20 yards away, his buckskin-clad form a light patch against the dark background of the forest.

Blade's eyes narrowed. The gunman would pass ten yards from his position, and was coming around the far side of the low rise. Blade's fingers probed the ground around him, and his left hand closed on a jagged piece of stone. He swept his hand up and back, and hurled the stone in a wide arc, over the low rise, over the advancing gunman and into the trees beyond.

There was a muffled crackling and thumping as the stone crashed through the leaves and bounced from limb to limb.

Hickok stopped and spun, facing the forest, his back to the rise.

Blade was up and running, his powerful legs churning, sprinting up the rise and reaching the top in four mighty strides. He launched himself into the air, his muscular arms outstretched, certain of victory. But even as his moccasined feet left the ground, he saw Hickok starting to turn, saw the gunman's right hand flashing toward his right Python. Hickok wore a matched pair of pearl-handled Colts strapped around his waist, and his prowess with the irons was legendary.

Hickok almost won.

The right Python was just clearing leather when Blade tackled his friend, his arms encircling the gunman and pinning Hickok's forearms, the force of his leap bearing them to the dank earth. He landed on top, astraddle the gunman.

Surprisingly, Hickok was taking his defeat calmly. He was on his left side, neither protesting nor squirming.

"Looks like I won this round," Blade commented, smirking.

"I don't know about that, pard," Hickok responded. "I think this is a draw."

"How do you figure?" Blade asked.

"Let me put it to you this way," Hickok said. "How do you feel about partin' with your family jewels?"

Blade glanced down.

Somehow, even as he fell, even with his arms pinned, Hickok had twisted his right hand, had angled the Python barrel around and in, the .357 Magnum pointing directly at Blade's gonads.

"I wouldn't sneeze if I were you," Hickok joked. "My hardware has a hair trigger."

Blade stood, smiling. "Not bad. But I still beat you to the punch. You fell for one of the oldest tricks in the book."

Hickok rose, holstering his right Colt. "Let me guess. You tossed a rock into the trees?"

"You got it," Blade said.

Hickok shrugged. "Well, you win some, you lose some. That's life."

"I never would have won," Blade stated, "if you hadn't cheated."

Hickok stared at his giant companion. "Let me get this straight. *You* won, and *I* cheated?"

"Don't play innocent with me," Blade said. "You were making enough noise to wake the dead. You wanted me to win. You wanted to get this over with so you can get home."

Hickok grinned sheepishly. "I figured if I made enough noise, you'd get overconfident, get careless, and do something stupid."

"I don't buy it," Blade told him.

"You don't?" Hickok responded. "Why not?"

"How long have I known you?" Blade queried.

Hickok frowned. "It's bad enough bein' second-guessed by my missus all the time! Don't you start too!"

Blade smiled. "Being outfoxed by your better half is normal in any marriage."

"Don't I know it!" Hickok exclaimed. "They're tricky, them female types! Before you tie the knot, they act so sweet and innocent. But after you're hitched, watch out! If you ask me, women make better drillmasters than men!"

Blade nodded. "Tell you what. Let's head on back. We can

finish this tomorrow night.''

"Tomorrow night?" Hickok responded in surprise. "Why are we comin' out here tomorrow night?"

"To make up for your lack of cooperation tonight," Blade informed him, grinning.

"You mean just 'cause I fudged a mite on one of the drills, we're goin' to do it all over again tomorrow night?" Hickok asked.

"You catch on real quick." Blade turned, walking to the north-west.

Hickok fell in alongside the head Warrior, grumbling.

"What did you say?" Blade asked.

The gunfighter glanced at Blade. "You *are* gettin' worse than my wife! You're turnin' into a real hardass."

"You think so?" Blade questioned.

"I know so!" Hickok stated. "And I ain't the only one who's noticed either. Geronimo, Rikki, and a few of the others have commented about it."

Now it was Blade's turn to display surprise. "You're serious?"

"You bet I am," Hickok said, looping his thumbs in his gunbelt. "You've changed, pard. I don't rightly know how best to describe it. You're more hard-nosed than before. Don't get me wrong. You were never exactly Little Bo Peep. But you changed after that business in Colorado. At least, you started to change. Everybody saw it. And it was confirmed on the last run you took, the one with Sundance and Bertha to Philadelphia.''

"The trip to Philadelphia wasn't any different than any of the missions we've been on together," Blade said.

"That's where you're wrong, pard," Hickok said, disagreeing. "It was a heap different. Sundance told us all about it. About how Bertha up and vanished, and instead of lookin' for her, you went on with the mission.''

Blade shrugged. "What's so unusual about that? We had an assignment, and the mission came first."

Hickok stared up at his friend. "It did then, that's for sure. You were all business. And that's my point. In the old days, before your tussle with Sammy in Denver, you always considered the mission as secondary. *We* came first! The Warriors with you were your first priority. Do you remember Thief River Falls? The Twin Cities? When any of us were in trouble, you dropped everything else and came to our aid. If we were hurt, you'd postpone the mission. Do you remember those times?"

Blade pondered the gunman's assertions, realizing Hickok was right. "I remember," he said slowly. "How could I forget them?"

"So what happened? Why the big change?" Hickok asked.

"I'm not sure if I can answer that," Blade replied. "I don't know if I know the answer."

"I ain't complainin', mind you," Hickok mentioned. "You've got a big load to carry, bein' top Warrior and all. You've got to be tough as nails."

Blade gazed at the trail they were following, his brow creased. "I think maybe it started during our Denver campaign, just like you said. That's when it dawned on me."

"What did?" Hickok inquired.

"The magnitude of our responsibility," Blade elaborated. "I'd always appreciated how important our job is, how necessary the Warriors are to the Family's survival. I recognized the fact intellectually. But I don't think I felt it, really experienced what I already knew, until the Home was attacked and almost destroyed. When Geronimo came to Denver and told us you were under assault, I was shocked. Horrified. Afraid you would be wiped out before we could reach you." He looked at the gunman. "You have no idea what it felt like. I finally understood—fully understood—how critical our conduct is to the Family's welfare and safety. If we slip up, the consequences can be disastrous! We must treat every mission as the most important thing in our lives. The Family's security depends on our performance, on our judgment. We can't let them down."

"So that explains the big change," Hickok said. "I'll have to tell the others. Everybody had a different idea as to what was goin' on."

"What did they think?" Blade asked.

"Geronimo said it was married life gettin' to you," Hickok revealed, and laughed. "Rikki felt it might be the strain takin' its toll."

"And how about you? What did you think?" Blade queried.

"Me?" Hickok grinned. "I just reckoned you had a corncob stuck up your butt."

"I knew I could count on you for an insightful analysis," Blade quipped.

"Hey! What are friends for?" Hickok retorted.

Blade, smiling, went to rest his hands on his Bowie hilts. He abruptly stopped in mid-stride. "Damn!"

Hickok halted. "What's wrong?"

"It's gone."

"What's gone?" Hickok inquired.

"My left Bowie," Blade said, tapping the empty sheath on his left hip. The right Bowie was secure in its scabbard.

"Where could it have gone?" Hickok asked, glancing over his left shoulder at the trail behind them.

Blade reflected for a moment. "I'll bet it fell out when I tackled you."

Hickok started to turn. "Then let's go look for it. I know you can't go beddy-bye without 'em tucked under your pillow."

"Thanks," Blade said, "but you head on back. I'll find the Bowie myself."

"I don't mind helpin' you," Hickok persisted.

"I know," Blade stated. "I appreciate the thought. But I don't want to hold you up. Head on home and tuck in Ringo."

"I don't know," Hickok said doubtfully.

Blade began retracing their path. "What? I can't find a knife by myself? I need you to hold my hand?"

"I don't mind helpin'," Hickok reiterated.

Blade waved the gunman off. "Go give Sherry a big kiss for me. It won't take more than a few minutes for me to find my knife. Go!"

"All right," Hickok remarked. "If that's what you want. But I'm tellin' you right here and now, pard, that if I give my missus a big kiss, it won't be for you!" He grinned, then wheeled, waving. "I'll see you tomorrow."

"Good night," Blade said. He hurried along their back trail, eager to find the Bowie and head on home. The thought of Jenny and little Gabe waiting for him, with a pot of venison stew boiling on their cast-iron stove, heightened his anticipation.

The leaves in the nearby trees were rustling with the breeze.

Blade mused on his good fortune as he jogged. He thanked the Spirit he'd been born in the Home, and had been reared under the beneficial influence of the Family. When he thought of the conditions existing outside the Home, of the savage barbarism rampant since World War III and the collapse of civilization, he felt intensely grateful for his lot in life. His frequent missions beyond the walled security of the Home only served to strengthen his conviction and increase his sense of thanksgiving. Only someone who knew what it was like to go without home and family, the two fundamental institutions of human society, he reasoned, could properly comprehend their importance. He'd seen the outside world, with all of its violence, with devious degenerates ready to murder without provocation, ready to slash someone's throat for the mere "thrill" of killing, and he hadn't liked what he'd seen. His philosophical musings came to an end as he rounded a large boulder and saw the low rise.

And something else.

Or someone else.

A towering figure stood at the base of the rise, a figure at least seven feet tall and solidly built, attired in a peculiar silver garment and silvery boots. The figure extended its right arm. "Do you seek this?" it asked in precise, clipped English.

Despite the gloom, Blade could distinguish the silver figure's rugged, yet oddly pale, features. A square jaw was capped by prominent cheekbones. Its eyes were an indeterminate color. Curly blond hair crowned its head.

"Do you seek this, Blade?" the figure repeated. It held its right arm aloft.

The silver garbed form was holding the missing Bowie.

"Who are you?" Blade demanded, taking a step forward, his right hand on his right Bowie. "How did you get in here? How do you know my name?"

"My name is AS-1," the figure stated imperiously. "And I was instructed to relay a message."

"Message?" Blade repeated, puzzled. "What are you babbling about?"

AS-1 lowered his right arm. "I am incapable of babbling," he said. "As for the message, it is simply this: Clarissa sends her regards."

"Who?"

"Clarissa," AS-1 said.

"I don't know any Clarissa," Blade declared.

"But she knows you," AS-1 disclosed. "And Primator sent us to retrieve you. Please do not resist."

Blade drew his right Bowie. "You're got it backwards, mister. You're coming with me. Make it easy on yourself and don't do anything stupid."

"My I.Q. is one hundred forty," AS-1 remarked. "It is impossible for me to commit a stupid act." He glanced to the left. "Take him."

Blade saw them coming out of the corner of his right eye. A pair of huge forms hurtling from the darkness, springing at him. He spun, dodging to the left, sidestepping their onslaught, his right arm a blur as he whipped the Bowie up and in, imbedding the knife to the hilt in the chest of one of his attackers. He wrenched the knife free as they plunged past him.

They stopped and whirled in concert, charging, not missing a beat. Tall forms dressed all in silver.

Blade braced himself, amazed the one he'd stabbed was still erect. They plowed into him in unison, one from the left, the other from the right, lifting him from the ground and slamming him onto his back, the brutal impact causing the air to whoosh from his lungs. He gasped and swung his left fist, clipping one of the silver men on the chin, expecting his foe to be knocked aside.

Instead, the silver man shook his head once, then stared at Blade and grinned.

Blade's mind was screaming a silent warning. Something was wrong here. Terribly, terribly wrong. He sensed it, his intuition blaring, and he surged against his adversaries. They were on their knees, one on each side, attempting to clamp their hands on his arms, to restrain him. Concentrating as they were on his arms, they failed to pin his legs. Blade took instant advantage of their neglect, sweeping his legs up, touching his knees to his chin and then lashing his legs out and down, catching the two silver men off guard, his legs clubbing them in the chest and sending them sprawling. He scrambled to his feet.

"Get him!" AS-1 ordered, still standing near the rise.

The two silver men came up in a rush, arms outstretched.

Blade twisted to the right, avoiding the nearest antagonist, and executed a wicked slicing arc with his right Bowie. The keen blade bit into the left wrist of the closest silver man, into the wrist and through the wrist.

The silver man's left hand dropped to the ground.

One out of the way! Grinning, Blade began to turn toward the second figure.

That was when the first assailant straightened and raised his severed forearm to his face, calmly examining the injured limb.

Blade, stunned, froze. He could see liquid pulsing from the ruined arm, but there wasn't enough of it, not the copious quantity there should be, and the silver man was reacting too placidly, was actually gazing at Blade with an air of serene resignation. Blade abruptly realized the silver man with the severed hand was the same one he'd stabbed in the chest. But that was impossible! No man could take such punishment, could receive two potentially fatal wounds, and be so unruffled by the injuries! What *were* these silver men?

"You were told not to resist," said a voice behind the Warrior.

Blade pivoted, knowing he'd blundered by forgetting the one near the rise, the one with his other Bowie. He attempted to bring his own knife into play, but something smashed into his right temple, staggering him, sending waves of agony rippling over his consciousness. He tottered, and almost fell. With a supreme effort, he was able to stay on his feet. But not for long. Another blow descended on his temple, and he felt his knees buckle as he collapsed, sprawling onto his hands and shins. The world was spinning. He struck out wildly with his Bowie, but missed.

A hard object collided with his temple for yet a third time, and the Family's head Warrior toppled forward into the dirt.

"He is ours," AS-1 stated.

# 3

Hickok heard the three voices before he saw the speakers. He recognized the distinctive vocal traits instantly.

" . . . agreed to drop the subject, yes?" said the first speaker.

"I didn't agree to drop nothin'!" snapped the second speaker in a lisping, high-pitched voice. "You bozos did all the agreeing!"

"We had to," asserted the third speaker, his tone low and raspy. "We knew we'd never hear the end of it otherwise."

"You still ain't heard the last of it!" stated the second speaker angrily.

Hickok was traveling a well-defined trail toward the western half of the Home. He walked past a row of pine trees and there they were, seated in the center of a small clearing, so involved in their argument, so wrapped up in the heat of their dispute, that their normally acute senses hadn't detected his approach. But they spotted him the moment he stepped into view, and one of them jumped up.

"Hickok! You startled Gremlin, yes?" the nervous one exclaimed.

"Howdy, Gremlin," Hickok said, greeting him, then nodding at the other two. "What are you yahoos doin'? Holdin' a powwow?"

"Powwow? Gremlin has never heard of a powwow, no," Gremlin said. He stood about five feet ten, and his skin was a leathery gray. Except for a brown loincloth, he was naked. His facial features were hawk-like, his noise pointed, his ears small circles of flesh, and his mouth was a mere slit. The eyes in his bald head contained eerie, stark red pupils. "What is a powwow, yes?"

25

"He means shootin' the breeze," stated the second of the three in his high-pitched voice. This one, when standing, stood under four feet in height, and he weighed only 60 pounds. His bony physique was covered with a coat of short, grayish-brown fur, and his face was decidedly feline in aspect: green, slanted eyes, pointed ears, and a curved forehead, just like a cat's. His fingernails were long and tapered to points. Like Gremlin, he wore a loincloth, but his was gray.

"So what are you guys doin', Lynx?" Hickok asked the cat-man.

"What's it to you?" Lynx retorted.

"Ignore him, Hickok," advised the third member of the trio. "He's in a bad mood. Again," he added in his low tone.

"What's got Lynx riled this time, Ferret?" Hickok inquired, moving over to join them.

Ferret was only an inch taller than Lynx. He wore a black loincloth. His whole body was encased in a coat of brown hair, three inches in length. His head resembled that of his namesake, with an extended nose and tiny brown eyes. His nose constantly twitched. "The same thing he's been upset about for months," he answered.

"What's that?" Hickok questioned.

"Fitting in," Ferret said.

"I don't follow you," Hickok mentioned.

"What's to follow?" Lynx interjected, annoyed. "I want to fit in around here, is all."

Hickok glanced at Gremlin and Ferret. "But you guys do fit in. Has anyone in the Family given you a hard time 'bout livin' here?"

"No," Lynx responded. "But they wouldn't pipe up even if they didn't like us. Your Family is so sicky-sweet and lovey-dovey, spreadin' kindness and love all over the place, they wouldn't say anything to hurt our feelings."

The gunman studied the cat-man. "If no one's objected to you bein' here, what's the beef?"

Lynx's feline features rippled as he struggled to repress his surging emotions. He was obviously furious over something, and was striving to keep his fury in check. "Would you *really* like to know what's buggin' me?"

Hickok nodded. "I'd really like to know," he answered sincerely.

Lynx pointed at Gremlin and Ferret, then tapped his furry chest. "We're not like the rest of you. Or ain't you noticed?"

"You're mutants. Big deal," Hickok said. "The world is crawlin' with mutants since the Big Blast."

"We're genetically engineered mutations!" Lynx stated angrily. "And that makes us different than all the rest." He swept his right arm in a wide arc. "All the other mutations out there are the result of all the radiation and chemicals and who-knows-what-else dumped on the environment during World War III. But we came from a test-tube, Hickok! A lousy test-tube! The damn Doktor created us in his lab! Took ordinary human embryos and turned 'em into us!" Lynx clenched his hands into compact fists. "Freaks! That's what we are! Nothin' more than freaks!" He paused. "You know, I heard test-tube babies were a big deal before the war. I heard the scientists were experimenting with all types of genetically engineered creatures. Slicing genes and all kinds of crap like that. The Doktor just took their work one step further. He wanted to create his own little personal assassin corps. Intelligent pets to do his bidding! That's why the bastard made us!"

"But you rebelled," Hickok reminded the fiery feline.

Lynx snorted derisively. "Fat lot of good it did us! Oh, sure, we survived when the rest of the Doc's Genetic Research Division was destroyed. And it was real kind of your Family to take us in for helpin' you out. But . . ."

"But what?" Hickok prodded.

"But what have we done since?" Lynx demanded. "We do some huntin' for you, and odd jobs now and then, and play with the munchkins. That's it!"

"What's wrong with that?" Hickok asked. "Sounds to me like you've got it easy."

"We do," Lynx admitted. "But I'm tired of havin' it easy. I was bred for action, Hickok. I'm a natural-born fighter, just like you and Blade and Rikki and the rest of the Warriors. And part of me is human, and my human part wants to do something constructive with my life. Something worthwhile. I want to contribute my fair share to the Family, repay you for your hospitality. I want to fit in."

"So that's what you meant," Hickok said.

Lynx took a step toward the gunfighter. "You can help us, Hickok."

"How?" Hickok asked. He could guess the answer. Blade and he were both aware of the ongoing dispute the mutants were having over Lynx's not-so-secret desire. And, as Blade had rightly pointed out, it was up to the mutants to broach the subject first.

"Shhhhhh!" Gremlin suddenly hissed, glancing skyward.

"What is it?" Ferret inquired.

"Gremlin heard something, yes," Gremlin told them.

Hickok looked at the tallest genetic deviate. Gremlin was the antsy type, highly emotional. But he was loyal to a fault, and his eyesight and hearing were superb. During Gremlin's youth, while at the Citadel in Cheyenne, Wyoming, the Doktor had performed an exploratory operation on Gremlin's brain as part of the Doktor's continual upgrading of his medical knowledge and expertise. The Doktor had removed a portion of Gremlin's brain as an experiment. The result was Gremlin's unorthodox speech pattern.

"I didn't hear nothin'," Lynx said.

"You were talking," Ferret noted. "And I was listening to you. Did you hear anything, Hickok?"

The gunman shook his head.

"Gremlin heard something!" Gremlin insisted. "We must investigate, no?"

"You investigate," Lynx said. "I want to finish talkin' to Hickok."

"If Gremlin goes," Ferret stated, "we all go. Isn't that what we pledged? You were the one who read *The Three Musketeers* in the Family library, remember? One for all and all for one. Right?"

"Yeah," Lynx responded, frowning. He gazed at Gremlin. "What did you hear?"

"Gremlin's not certain, yes?" Gremlin replied, his red eyes staring to the east. "Funny kind of buzzing, no?"

"Maybe it was a giant mosquito," Hickok quipped, only partially in jest. Certain insect strains had developed tendencies toward inexplicable giantism since the war, growing to immense proportions.

"Not mosquito, no," Gremlin asserted. "Something different, yes?"

"Let's go find the damned thing!" Lynx snapped. He faced the gunfighter. "Why don't you come along? I'd like to talk with you some more."

Hickok hesitated, thinking of his waiting wife and son.

"Please," Lynx persisted.

Hickok's eyes narrowed. He'd never heard Lynx ask anything so politely before. Lynx must consider it very important indeed. And he could hardly refuse Lynx, because he still owed all three of the mutants for saving his wife's life. "I'll stick with you a spell," he declared. "But let's get this over with. I've got to get home."

Gremlin led them into the trees, bearing to the east. Lynx came next, then Hickok and Ferret.

Hickok marveled at their incredibility silent passage through the vegetation. He was only a few feet away, but couldn't hear a sound.

Gremlin increased his speed, and Lynx kept pace.

Ferret caught up with Hickok and nudged the gunman's right elbow. "You're not mad at Lynx, are you?" he whispered.

"No," Hickok answered softly. "Why should I be?"

"Lynx has a way of getting people upset," Ferret said. "He can be too blunt at times, too inconsiderate. Especially when he's in a bad mood, like now."

"I'll hear him out," Hickok promised. "If he needs my help, I'll do what I can. I'm not forgettin' what you guys did for my missus."

"That was last October," Ferret mentioned. "This is April."

"A debt is a debt," Hickok stated. "Any hombre who doesn't pay his debts ain't much of a man in my book. The same holds true for women."

"We could use your assistance," Ferret remarked. "We want—"

"Shhhh!" came from Gremlin, ten yards ahead.

Hickok crouched. Ferret passed him, stooped over, and he followed. They reached a cluster of bushes and found Gremlin and Lynx on their knees, gaping at an object in a large clearing beyond. Hickok peeked over the top of the bushes, wondering if it was a wild animal, or one of the bizarre ravenous mutations, or even raiders who had somehow managed to scale the outer wall and swim the inner moat. His mind contemplated every possibility in the space of several seconds, his hands on his Colts, thinking he was prepared for anything.

He was wrong.

The gunman's mouth dropped at the sight of the enormous craft in the clearing, a huge black aircraft of advanced design. Hickok racked his memory, attempting to recall the books in the Family library dealing with aviation. He'd read many of them as a child, entranced by the technological accomplishments of prewar society. The Family's Founder had stocked the library with hundreds of thousands of volumes on every conceivable subject. The books containing photographs were especially prized by members of the Family, fascinated as they were by any glimpse of their ancestors' civilization. Although many of the old volumes were faded or yellowed with age and required diligent care when handled, the Family members perused them avidly. Hickok had seen dozens of photographs of ancient aircraft. He'd even seen a functional jet once, and helicopters. But never a craft like the one before him.

"What is it?" Ferret blurted, amazed.

"It ain't no mosquito," Lynx said.

Gremlin turned toward Hickok. "You are Warrior, yes? What we do is up to you, no?"

Hickok peered at the aircraft. The strange vehicle was more than 20 yards away, too far to discern much detail. What was the craft doing there? he asked himself. Why was it in the Home? And who was flying the thing? Why had they landed in the dead of night? Sabotage? A spy mission? What?

"Come on, chuckles!" Lynx urged him. "Let's check this sucker out!"

"I should let Blade know about this," Hickok whispered.

"Can't any of you Warriors take a leak without Blade aimin' your pecker?" Lynx retorted.

Hickok slowly stood. The craft was quiet, and no one was in sight. He could see a doorway of some sort near the nose of the craft. The door was ajar, permitting a greenish light to illuminate a rectangular area under the nose.

"Are you makin' up your mind, or did you fall asleep?" Lynx queried sarcastically.

"We'll take a look," Hickok said, "but you three stay behind me." He drew his Pythons.

Lynx rose. "We don't need you to baby-sit us!" he said indignantly.

Hickok spun. "I'm the Warrior here! And in times of danger, the Warriors are in charge! For all we know, that thing could pose a threat to the Family! So if you want to come, come! But you do what I say, when I tell you! Got it?"

Lynx grinned. "Anyone ever tell you how cute you are when you're pissed off?"

Hickok turned toward the craft, then carefully advanced through the bushes to the clearing. He distinguished three immense wheels supporting the aircraft, one under the nose, and one under each wing. The wings were configured differently from those on the jet he'd seen. They began about a third of the distance from the nose, then flared out to form a gigantic triangular shape. They vaguely resembled those on a military craft in one of the books in the library, and he recalled a term he'd read: delta wing. A faint greenish light was visible under the canopy. And big white letters had been painted on the side.

Lynx came up on the gunman's left. "I ain't seen nothin' like that before," he said. "Not in the Civilized Zone, not with the Doktor, not anywhere."

"Neither have I, pard," Hickok remarked, his keen blue eyes sweeping the aircraft and the surrounding terrain. He angled toward the doorway, reflecting. How long had the craft been there? How could such a big thing have landed without being spotted? Jets and helicopters made a heap of noise. So why hadn't anyone heard the craft in front of him? The ominous black aircraft was distinctly unsettling, and the implications of its presence worried him.

"Do you want one of us to sneak inside and see what's in there?" Lynx queried in a whisper.

"If anyone goes in there," Hickok replied, "it'll be me. You just do what I tell you."

"Yes, *sir!*" Lynx rejoined.

Hickok gazed along the length of the mystery craft. He

estimated the aircraft was a minimum of 40 yards long. The wing span was difficult to gauge because of the darkness. He surveyed the edge of the clearing, perplexed. A ring of trees and brush surrounded the clearing. Didn't jets require a lot of space to take off or land? So how the blazes had this black craft descended? Straight down? He shut all speculation from his mind as he neared the doorway, located 15 yards from the nose.

"What's that mean?" Lynx asked, pointing at the side of the aircraft.

Hickok glanced at the white lettering. ANDROXIA.

"What's Androxia?" Lynx questioned.

"You're askin' me?" Hickok responded. He cautiously approached the doorway. The door was open several inches.

"Perhaps we should knock, yes?" Gremlin inquired from behind the gunman.

"Are you crazy?" Lynx said. "We don't know who's in there." He deliberately paused. "Unless, of course, *Mr.* Hickok wants to knock."

"I'd like to knock your block off," Hickok quipped. He reached the door.

"I'd like to see you try!" Lynx countered.

"Children! Please!" Ferret spoke up. "This is not the time or place."

"Ferret speaks the truth, yes?" Gremlin added. "You two stop bickering, no?"

"Who's bickering?" Lynx responded.

"Will all of you *shut up*?" Hickok hissed. "How can I sneak inside with you three idiots flappin' your gums?"

"Who are you callin' an idiot?" Lynx demanded.

"Go find a mirror," Hickok retorted, and eased the metal door open.

The interior of the craft was lit by a greenish light emanating from recessed translucent squares in the ceiling. A narrow passage ran from the doorway to another, wider corridor.

"You three stay put," Hickok stated. "I'm goin' in."

No one said a word.

Hickok crept into the aircraft. He was surprised to find panelling on the walls and carpeting underfoot. A row of doors lined the left side of the passage. On an impulse, Hickok reached out and yanked on the latch of the second door he passed. The door swung out, revealing four silver uniforms hanging from a rack. On the shoulders of each uniform, enclosed in a circle, was that word again: ANDROXIA. He closed the door and hurried to the connecting corridor.

"Which way?"

Hickok whirled.

Lynx and Ferret were right behind him.

"I thought I told you to stay put!" Hickok growled.

"Don't lay an egg!" Lynx advised. "Gremlin is keepin' watch."

Hickok reined in his raging temper. He intended to settle the matter with the cantankerous feline at the first opportunity, but as Ferret had noted, now was not the time or place. He grit his teeth and took a right, heading toward the nose of the craft.

Lynx and Ferret padded on his heels.

Hickok passed four more doors. The corridor apparently ran the length of the craft. It widened slightly as it neared the nose, and suddenly they were in the spacious cockpit. A large canopy was overhead. Three cushioned seats were positioned in the middle of the cockpit, facing a complicated array of electronic components.

"That's a computer!" Ferret exclaimed. "The Doktor used them all the time."

"What are all those blinkin' lights?" Hickok asked.

"I don't know," Ferret admitted. "I saw the Doktor use his, but I wasn't taught how to use them."

"All that bastard taught us was how to kill," Lynx remarked. "As if we needed lessons!"

"The pilot isn't here," Hickok declared. "We'd best alert the Family."

"I'll go find Blade," Ferret offered.

"Good idea," Hickok concurred. "The last time I saw him, he was south of here a ways, lookin' for a Bowie he lost."

"I'll find him," Ferret stated. He turned.

Footsteps sounded in the corridor, the noise of someone in a hurry. Gremlin appeared at the junction, saw them, and raced to the cockpit. "They're coming!" he blurted in alarm. "They're coming, yes!"

"Calm down, dimwit!" Lynx barked. "Who's coming?"

"Men in gleaming clothes, yes!" Gremlin exclaimed. "Gremlin

saw them, yes!''

"How far away are they?" Hickok asked.

"Don't know, no!" Gremlin replied. "Gremlin saw them coming through trees to south, yes! Maybe a hundred yards, yes!''

"Then it'll take 'em a minute or two to get here," Hickok said, calculating. "We can surprise 'em."

"Did you see their faces?" Ferret inquired. "Are you sure they're men, Gremlin? Are you sure they're human?"

"Gremlin did not see faces, no," Gremlin answered. "What else could they be, yes?"

"We'll soon find out," Hickok stated. "Find a place to hide."

"One more thing, yes!" Gremlin said.

"What is it?" Hickok queried, searching the cockpit for a suitable hiding place.

"They carry someone, yes!" Gremlin told them.

"They're carryin' someone?" Hickok repeated.

"Are you certain?" Ferret inquired.

Gremlin nodded. "Gremlin certain, yes."

"You saw them carrying someone that far off?" Lynx chimed in. "I know we've got good eyesight, but—"

Gremlin's red eyes narrowed. "Gremlin saw them, yes! Don't call Gremlin liar, no!"

"I ain't callin' you a lair, you ding-a-ling!" Lynx said.

"Find a spot to hide!" Hickok ordered. "And don't nobody make a move unless I give the word."

"Can I wee-wee without permission?" Lynx cracked flippantly.

Hickok ignored the cat-man and turned to a row of doors. He opened the first one. Inside was a closet containing a pile of boxes and a strange metal instrument, a square affair with a dozen switches and dials. There was plenty of space to the left of the pile, and he holstered his Pythons and quickly eased inside. "Hurry!" he declared, then closed the door. Darkness enveloped him. He could hear the others scurrying to concealment. A door opened to his right, and he knew one of them was using the next closet to hide. He was about to ask who it was, when he heard a voice whispering.

"Gremlin doesn't like this, no! Not one bit, yes!"

Hickok grinned. He lifted his right hand and rested it on his right Colt. There wasn't much room to maneuver, but he was confident he could draw if necessary. He debated a course of action. Should he confront these jokers as soon as they returned? Or should he wait, bide his time, eavesdrop on them, and possibly learn what they were up to, why they were at the Home? He opted for the second plan.

There was a muffled thump from the cockpit, from the direction of the computer, as if someone had bumped something.

"Damn computer!" Lynx muttered.

Hickok smiled. It served the runt right! Lynx was normally a feisty critter, but he'd never seen Lynx as touchy as tonight. He'd known something was bothering the feline for months, but Lynx hadn't said a word to any of the Family about the cause. On numerous occasions he'd seen Lynx and the other two engaged in intense arguments. Lynx seemed to be taking one side, Ferret and Gremlin the other. Hickok had a notion why they were spatting, but he hadn't wanted to . . .

Somewhere, a door slammed.

Hickok waited expectantly.

There was an exchange of muted voices.

Hickok fingered the trigger on his right Python.

" . . . immediately. Primator will be pleased," said a deep voice, the audibility increasing as the speaker neared the cockpit.

"I was impressed," said a second person. "He is quite formidable."

Hickok pressed his right ear to the door panel. Oddly enough, the two voices were almost, but not quite, identical.

"I'm proof of that," commented yet a third party.

The unknown trio reached the cockpit, and there was a commotion as they went about their business.

"How much coolant have you lost?" asked one of them.

"Two quarts," answered another.

"Go to the Wells Repair Module," instructed the first voice. "I will perform emergency crimping on your tubes. It will suffice until we reach Androxia."

"Thank you," said the other one. "I will place my hand in the Boulle to prevent excessive dehydration."

What the blazes were they talking about? Hickok wondered.

"If his knife had penetrated your Heinlein, you would require a major overhaul," commented the third one. He paused. "Should

Blade be placed in stasis?''

Blade! They had Blade! Hickok felt a slight vibration under his feet as he gripped the latch and shoved. He leaped from the closet, his thumb on the hammer of his right Python. ''Don't move!'' he shouted, whipping his right Colt up and out, then stopping, stupefied.

There were three of them, each seven feet in height, each attired in a silver uniform. They all had blond hair, blue eyes, and pale skin. They looked enough alike to be triplets. One stood in front of the computer. The second one, with Blade's unconscious form draped over his left shoulder, was standing five feet to the left of the gunman. The third giant was near the doorway, a ragged tear in his uniform in the center of his chest, a pale fluid seeping from the hole, *holding his severed left hand in his right!*

The one near the computer glanced at the one holding Blade. ''You were correct. You did observe someone near the Hoverjet.''

''I'll do the talkin'!'' Hickok snapped. He wagged his Python at the one with Blade. ''You! Set my pard on the floor! Nice and easy like!''

To the gunman's astonishment, his command was ignored. The one with Blade looked at the one near the computer. ''This must be another Warrior. Should we dispose of him?''

''I believe this is the organism called Hickok,'' remarked the silver man near the door. ''I'm familiar with primitive firearms, and those are Colt Pythons. He is an associate of Blade's.''

''Then we will transport him to Androxia,'' the one by the computer stated.

''You ain't transportin' me nowhere!'' Hickok declared. ''This contraption of yours is stayin' right on the ground!''

''That's impossible,'' the one near the computer stated.

''Wanna bet?'' Hickok rejoined, pointing his Python at the man's head.

''We do not gamble,'' the silver man said. ''And we can not stay on the ground when we are already in the air.'' He motioned toward the canopy.

Hickok risked a hasty glance upward. He could see the stars, and they were moving! With a start, he suddenly realized the stars weren't really moving: *the aircraft was!* They were airborne!

The silver man near the computer scrutinized the gunman's

expression. "We departed your Home over a minute ago. Our onboard navigational computer automatically implemented our takeoff. The Klinecraft is soundproofed, and motion fluctuation is minimal. There was no way you could have known."

"Turn this buggy around!" Hickok demanded. "You're takin' us back."

"No, we are not," said the one by the computer, and he nodded at the silver man near the doorway.

Hickok whirled.

The one with the cut-off hand was already charging, his right arm upraised to deliver a crushing blow.

Hickok's right Python boomed, thundering in the confines of the cockpit. As he invariably did, Hickok went for the head. He was a staunch advocate of always going for the brain. If an opponent was hit anywhere else, they could keep coming. Even if a foe was shot in the heart, they could linger for several seconds or longer, enough time to squeeze a trigger or get in a final swipe. But snuff the brain, as Hickok liked to say, and nine times out of ten the enemy was instantly slain. Nine times out of ten.

This time was the tenth.

The silver man was struck in the left eye, the impact of the 158-grain hollow-point slug jerking his massive body to the left and stopping him in his tracks. He hesitated for just a fraction, then plunged forward, seemingly immune to pain and heedless of the gaping cavity where his left eye had just been.

Hickok's Python blasted again. And once more. Each shot was on target. The first one caught the silver man in the forehead, snapping his head backward and blowing the rear of his cranium outward, spraying the cockpit wall and carpeted floor with grisly pieces of flesh and hair and spattering everything with a colorless liquid. The silver man halted, shook his head once, then resumed his attack. Hickok's next shot hit his assailant in the right eye.

The silver man doubled over, clutching at his shattered face, a watery substance spewing onto the floor.

Hickok was astounded. Never had he seen anyone take such punishment and still keep coming.

But this one did.

The silver man straightened, his arms extended. He had dropped his left hand, and the fingers on his right clawed at the air. His eyes were gone, yet he advanced, shuffling in the direction of the Warrior, his right arm swinging from side to side.

How the hell did he do it? Hickok sent two more slugs into the silver man's head.

The man in silver abruptly stiffened. His mouth curved downwards, his lips trembling. He took a single halting step, then collapsed in a heap.

Hickok couldn't accept the testimony of his own eyes.

Smoke was wafting from the dead man's ruined eye sockets!

The gunman's superb instincts sensed danger, and his left hand streaked to his left Colt as he pivoted to face the other two silver men. He almost made it.

The silver man near the computer had already sprung into action, executing a flying leap, his heavy form hurtling through the intervening space and crashing into the Warrior, slamming the gunman against the closet door, ramming the gunfighter's head into the door. The panel split from the force of the blow, and the gunman slumped to the green carpet, his right Python slipping from his limp fingers.

AS-1 rose to his full height and stared at the Warrior at his feet. "These Warriors are not to be taken lightly," he commented. "I will inform Intelligence upon our return to Androxia." He glanced at his crumpled companion. "OV-3's Bradbury Chip was struck by one of Hickok's shots," he deduced.

IM-97 transferred Blade from his left shoulder to his arms, then walked to the doorway. "I will place this one in stasis and return for Hickok."

AS-1 nodded. "I will transmit the status of our mission to Androxia."

IM-97 gazed at the body of OV-3. "How do you think Primator will react to the loss of a Superior?"

AS-1 nudged OV-3 with the tip of his right toe. "The humans have an expression," he remarked. "Apropos in this instance."

"What is it?" IM-97 inquired.

"The shit will hit the fan."

# 4

She stood on the balcony on the top floor of the Huxley Tower, her lavender eyes sweeping the skyline of Androxia.

Where were they?

She gazed at the city lights far below, then up at the heavens, idly noting the position of the Big Dipper.

They had to come!

They had to succeed!

Her flowing, oily black hair was whipped by the wind as she turned to the north. The wind felt cool on her scaly yellow skin. Her thin blue dress did little to protect her from the elements.

That bastard had to pay!

Had to reap his punishment for murdering the Doktor!

Her beloved Doktor!

She frowned at the recollection, the memories almost too agonizing to tolerate. She recalled the campaign the Doktor had waged against the accursed Family. She vividly remembered the final battle in Catlow, Wyoming. And tears welled in her eyes as she mentally reviewed the day after that last conflict, when she'd donned a grubby pair of jeans, an old brown shirt, and a tattered tan coat and, after stuffing her waist-length hair into a shabby cap, had ventured into Catlow at sunset, determined to learn the fate of her creator . . . and her lover.

Somewhere in Androxia, a siren wailed.

She'd viewed the battle from a nearby hill and watched, horrified, as the damned Warriors and their allies defeated the Doktor's Genetic Research Division, utterly wiped them out. So far as she knew, she was the only one remaining. And she wouldn't have survived, would have perished with the Doktor and

39

the rest, if her darling mentor hadn't ordered her to remain behind.

She sobbed.

The Doktor had felt uneasy about Catlow, had even speculated it was a trap. Was that the reason he'd left her behind? Was it because he'd wanted to spare her?

And to think!

She'd almost deserted him!

A lump formed in her throat as the bitter remembrance of her flight from Catlow overwhelmed her. She'd wanted to reach Denver as fast as possible, to demand Samuel II lead a counterstrike against Catlow. She'd gone 20 miles before she'd braked her jeep and done a U-turn, heading back to Catlow. Her intuition had told her the Doktor was dead, but she'd needed to ascertain the truth with her own eyes, to actually see his corpse, before she could accept the reality of his demise. She'd doubled back, concealed the jeep, stolen the clothing she needed from a deserted ranch house, and bravely sallied into Catlow as darkness descended.

And she'd found him.

Tears cascaded down her round cheeks.

The slime!

The fucking slime!

They'd hung the Doktor by his heels from a tree near the town square! And there they were, the inebriated residents of Catlow, celebrating their newfound independence, drinking and singing and mocking the Doktor. She'd walked among them, rage filling her being, and had listened to their banter, particularly to the conversation concerning the battle. And she'd learned what she'd needed.

The name of the Doktor's killer.

Blade.

Right then and there, she'd vowed to repay him, to revenge herself on the son of a bitch. A simple bullet was too good for the bastard. Her vengeance had to be special. Spectacular. She'd wanted Blade to suffer as no man had ever suffered before, and she still did.

Oh, how he'd pay!

She'd departed Catlow, returned to her jeep. And as she drove to the south, a new plan had formed in her devious mind. She'd realized Samuel II might not be equal to the task of destroying the Family, and subsequent events had confirmed her estimation. She'd known she couldn't achieve her revenge by her lonesome. She'd perceived she needed a better ally than Samuel II, and what better one than the Doktor's secret confederate in Androxia?

Who better than Primator?

She smiled, stifling the flow of tears, anticipating her impending triumph. It'd taken so long—so damn long—but she'd finally prevailed on Primator to assist her, had convinced him killing Blade was for the benefit of all Androxia.

And the fool had fallen for her ploy!

She thought of Blade writhing in torment as his body was lowered into a vat of molten steel, pleading for his life, and she cackled.

# 5

Was it safe yet?

Gremlin cautiously eased the closet door open and peeked outside. The cockpit was shrouded in silence, dimly lit with a greenish glow by the overhead lights. He craned his neck, examining every square inch, verifying the silver men were gone. Satisfied, he tentatively stepped from concealment, prepared to duck from sight at the slightest sound.

"Pssst!"

Gremlin involuntarily jumped, his red eyes widening in consternation.

"Pssst! Gremlin!" whispered a voice from near the computer. "Don't faint, you twit! It's me! Lynx!" So saying, Lynx emerged from hiding around the right side of the large navigational console. "It was cramped as all get-out back there," he complained.

Gremlin glanced at the doorway. "Does Lynx think they left, yes? Would not want to run into them again, no!"

Lynx crossed the cockpit and joined Gremlin. "Those morons are long gone."

"Where is Ferret, yes?" Gremlin asked.

"I'm right here," Ferret announced, coming through the doorway. "I hid in a compartment in the corridor. I saw them leave with Blade and Hickok."

"Poor Hickok, yes!" Gremlin exclaimed. "We should have helped him, no?"

"No," Lynx said.

"What happened in here?" Ferret inquired. "I heard all the gunshots, and I peeped out and saw one of those big guys carrying

42

Blade right past me. He came back and lugged Hickok away."

"They captured Hickok, yes!" Gremlin declared.

Ferret stared at Lynx. "And you did nothing to help?"

"Nope," Lynx admitted. "Why should I have helped him? Hickok told us not to move unless he gave the word." Lynx shrugged. "The dummy never gave the word."

"So you just sat there and did nothing?" Ferret asked accusingly.

"Hey! Don't look at me like that!" Lynx snapped. "I was following his orders! And I didn't just *sit* there. I was *lyin'* behind the computer."

Ferret shook his head in disapproval. "I can't believe you! You let them take him!"

"It all happened so fast, there wasn't much I *could* do," Lynx commented. "Besides, I didn't see you two lend a hand."

"Gremlin was in closet, yes," Gremlin remarked. "Gremlin didn't see what happened."

"Nor did I," Ferret said. "All I could see was a stretch of the hallway."

Lynx glanced at both of them. "What? Your ears ain't workin'? You couldn't tell Hickok was in trouble?"

Neither Ferret or Gremlin responded.

"Don't be pointing no finger at me!" Lynx mentioned. "At least I crawled out when the shootin' started. I saw them take him down." He paused. "There's something fishy about those characters. I don't think they're human. You should see the way they move. And Hickok's bullets didn't have much effect. So after they knocked him out, I crawled back behind the computer. I figured there wasn't much I could do, not until I learn more about these clowns."

Gremlin gazed out the canopy. Several hundred feet overhead was a corrugated metal ceiling. Fluorescent lights were suspended from chains at 20-foot intervals. "Where are we, yes?"

Ferret looked upward. "My guess would be in a hangar of some kind. But I wouldn't have the slightest idea where the hangar is located. We were in the air for a couple of hours. We could be anywhere."

"Who cares where we are?" Lynx said. "This is our golden opportunity!"

"Uh-oh," Ferret declared. "I don't like that gleam in your

eyes.''

"Don't you see?" Lynx queried. "This is the chance we need to get what we want!"

"Gremlin doesn't understand, no," Gremlin stated.

"I think I do," Ferret said. "And I'm not sure I like it."

Lynx leaned toward Gremlin. "Let me spell it out for you, pal. What were we talkin' about tonight before Hickok showed up?"

"The same old subject, yes," Gremlin said. "What to do with our lives, no?"

"Exactly," Lynx concurred. "What to do with our lives? How can we fit in at the Home? And what's the answer?"

"Gremlin doesn't know, yes," Gremlin responded.

"Well, *I* know," Lynx claimed. "And I've been tryin' to convince you dorks for months."

"It does seem like forever," Ferret quipped.

Lynx glared at Ferret, then smiled at Gremlin. "Look. We've been through this a zillion times. We want to fit in at the Home. We want to do something worthwhile with our lives. Right?"

"Yes," Gremlin replied.

"And the Doc bred us to be fighters, didn't he?" Lynx questioned. "I mean, fightin' is in our genes! Right?"

"Yes," Gremlin agreed.

"So if we're such naturally talented fighters, and if we like being at the Home and want to do something to help them out, then what better way than to become full-fledged Warriors! Right?" Lynx beamed.

"Wrong," Ferret answered.

"No," Gremlin said.

Lynx hissed. He placed his hands on his hips and stared at them defiantly. "What's wrong with my idea?"

"Everything," Ferret said. "Like you said, we've been through this already. Time and time again. Being a Warrior is a serious responsibility. You can't become one just because you crave a little action, because you want some excitement in your life."

"That's not the only reason I want to become a Warrior," Lynx averred.

"Oh? What are your other reasons?" Ferret asked.

"I like the Family," Lynx maintained. "I want to do my fair share, to repay them for everything they've done for us. Is that so bad?"

"No," Ferret said. "Not if you're sincere."

"And you don't think I am?" Lynx inquired.

"Let's just say I have my doubts," Ferret stated.

"Gremlin too, yes," Gremlin added.

Lynx exhaled noisily. "You two take the cake, you know that? Here I am, your best buddy in all the world, and you won't believe I can have an honest motive like everybody else. Fine! Be that way! I've spent months tryin' to convince you, to show you being Warriors is just right for us! We'd make great Warriors! We'd be happy, happier than we've been in ages! But no! You think I'm just being selfish." He paused, swept them with his green eyes. "Well, I'm done! I'm through tryin' to show you the error of your ways! I'm through tryin' to talk some sense into a pair of vacuum heads! If you don't want to be Warriors, terrific! But I do! And I'm gonna be one, with or without you! I'm not about to pass up a chance like this."

"What chance, yes?" Gremlin queried.

Lynx waved his left arm at the canopy. "*This* chance, bub! A golden opportunity to show the Family what we can do. Blade and Hickok are out there somewhere, prisoners. If we can save 'em, bail their butts out of this fix, we can write our own ticket. In order to become a Warrior, you have to be sponsored by a Warrior, right? So imagine how grateful Blade and Hickok will be after we save 'em. They'd do anything for us. Hickok already owes us for savin' his wife. All we'd have to do is ask, and I'll bet they'd gladly sponsor us for Warrior status. It'd be a breeze! But if you guys don't want to help, that's okay. I'll do it myself."

"Before you go running off half-cocked," Ferret said, "you should know there are a few flaws in your logic."

"Like what?" Lynx countered.

"Like you don't know where we are," Ferret said, beginning his enumeration. "You don't know if Blade or Hickok are still alive. Even if you succeed in rescuing them, how will you return to the Home? On foot? You have no idea of what you're going up against. And you have no guarantee Blade or Hickok will nominate you to become a Warrior."

"Why quibble over a few trifling details?" Lynx retorted.

"Trifling?" Ferret said. "They qualify as insurmountable difficulties."

"Only to a pessimist like you," Lynx said. "Look, are you

guys with me or not?''

Ferret sighed. "This won't be easy."

"What in life is easy?" Lynx rejoined.

"It's insane," Ferret commented.

"What other choice do we have?" Lynx demanded. "Do you just want to cut out on Blade and Hickok? Leave 'em in the lurch? We're the only chance they've got."

Ferret frowned, his hairy brow furrowed in thought. "No," he said after a spell. "We can't desert them. We must try and find them."

Lynx grinned. "Then let's go."

"We should have a plan, yes?" Gremlin interjected.

"Who needs a plan?" Lynx responded. "Just stick with me." He strolled from the cockpit.

Gremlin looked at Ferret. "We are in big trouble, yes?"

"You can stay here if you want," Ferret suggested. "I'll try and keep Lynx from getting himself killed."

Gremlin shook his head. "Gremlin come too. One for all and all for one, yes? Isn't that our motto, no?"

"Then let's go," Ferret said, turning to follow Lynx. "And let's hope we don't live to regret this."

Lynx was waiting for them at the junction with the passage to the door. "Come on, slowpokes!" he grumbled.

Gremlin and Ferret hastened to his side.

"We've gotta stick together," Lynx said. He pointed at the closed door. "We don't know what we'll find out there. Keep alert. And if we bump into those silver bozos, go for their nuts."

"Their nuts?" Ferret repeated, puzzled.

"Yeah. Their nuts. Balls. Coconuts. Whatever you want to call them," Lynx said.

"Why, pray tell, should we go for their testicles?" Ferret inquired.

"Two reasons," Lynx replied. "One, they're bigger than us. Way bigger. But their nuts are at just the right height, unless you'd rather nibble on their tootsies or jump up and tweak their noses."

"And what's the second reason?" Ferret asked.

"Going for the head doesn't seem to do much good," Lynx stated. "Hickok emptied one of his Colts into the head of one of those goons, and it hardly slowed the silver joker down."

"Hickok always aims for heads, yes," Gremlin mentioned.

"Yep. And Hickok ain't one to miss," Lynx observed. "Which goes to prove my point. Those silver guys ain't human."

"Perhaps they're superhuman," Ferret suggested.

"Then where's their scent?" Lynx demanded.

"Their scent?" Ferret responded in surprise.

"Yeah, dummy! Their scent!" Lynx said. "Brother! For someone who's got a nose as big as you do, you sure don't use it much! The Doc designed us with a great pair of sniffers. We can track anything by scent alone. Gremlin can't, 'cause he's a little more human than us."

"What about their scent, yes?" Gremlin queried.

"They don't have any," Lynx disclosed. "Not a trace. And humans always have a scent. So do animals."

Ferret's bewilderment at the revelation was evident in his face. "You're right!" he said to Lynx. "I didn't even notice!"

"See? I think all that easy livin' with the Family has made you rusty," Lynx stated. "You've heard that old sayin'. Use it or lose it."

Ferret frowned, displeased by his performance. If his normally acute senses had atrophied at the Home, it was a cause for concern. Within the walled 30-acre compound, where all the dangerous wild animals had been exterminated, where danger seldom threatened, where menace was not part of the daily routine, his full faculties were not essential to his survival. But out in the "real world," where the law of the jungle prevailed, where survival of the fittest was the standard, sharp senses were critical. They could mean the difference between life and death.

Lynx glanced at Gremlin. "Gremlin, keep your ears peeled. You've got the best hearing, so we'll rely on you to warn us if someone comes our way."

"Gremlin will not let you down, yes!" Gremlin vowed.

Lynx grinned. "Then let's go save Blade and Hickok, and whip some ass in the bargain." He moved along the passage to the door, then paused, listening. "I don't hear nothin'," he said. "Do you?" he asked Gremlin.

Gremlin shook his head. "Gremlin not hear any noise, any voices outside, no," he replied.

Lynx nodded, and slowly twisted the latch. The door opened with a faint snap. He carefully eased the door outward and peered around the edge. "Wow!" he exclaimed.

"What do you see?" Ferret asked.

Lynx glanced over his left shoulder. "It's incredible! I thought the Doc had a fancy setup. Take a gander at this." He moved aside.

Ferret stepped to the doorway and peeked past the door. His brown eyes widened in amazement.

The aircraft was parked in a hangar, as Ferret had earlier speculated, but the size, the sheer scope of the facility, was beyond his wildest imagining. The building was immense. The ceiling alone was 300 feet above the cement floor. Lengthwise, the structure covered 500 yards, and its width was half again as great. The aircraft was situated in one of the corners, its tail extended toward the middle of the hangar, according them an unobstructed view of the interior.

"Gremlin wants to take a look, yes?" Gremlin said.

Ferret retreated and stood next to Lynx. "What sort of technology are we dealing with here?" he asked in an awed voice.

"Even the Doc's lab, the Biological Center, was puny compared to this," Lynx commented.

"Where do we begin to search for Blade and Hickok?" Ferret inquired.

"We've got a problem there," Lynx conceded. "I can't pick up much of their scent."

"The Warriors were being carried," Ferret said. "Their feet weren't touching the ground."

"We'll find a way," Lynx predicted confidently.

Gremlin suddenly ducked from the doorway. "Someone is coming, yes!" he cried.

"Who is it?" Lynx asked.

"Another man dressed in silver, yes!" Gremlin told them.

"Did he see you?" Lynx asked.

Gremlin shook his head. "Gremlin doesn't think so, no!"

Lynx nodded at the row of doors lining the left side of the passage. "Quick! Each of us in a closet!"

The three genetic deviates hurried into hiding.

Not a moment too soon.

The outer door was abruptly wrenched all the way open, and a giant silver man entered the aircraft.

Lynx, his closet door deliberately left slightly ajar, saw the giant enter. The silver man was holding a clipboard in his left hand and he passed once inside and gazed at the doorway, as if perplexed at finding the door partially open. He turned and moved past the row of closets. Lynx could hear the giant's firm tread, and guessed the silver man had turned right at the junction and gone to the cockpit. What was the giant doing? Lynx wondered. Checking the aircraft after its flight? He slid from the closet and padded to the junction, then looked around the corner. Sure enough, the giant was in the cockpit, standing in front of the computer, studying a digital display and writing on a white pad affixed to the clipboard.

The giant's broad back was to the doorway.

Lynx padded down the corridor to the cockpit door, calculating his next move. Finding Blade and Hickok would be an easy task if they knew where to look, and it was possible the giant in the cockpit knew where the two Warriors were being held. Lynx resolved to force the giant to talk using whatever means were necessary. His feline instincts were warning him to vacate this place—wherever it might be—as quickly as feasible, and he wasn't one to argue with his instincts. But how, he asked himself, was he going to force the seven-foot giant to spill the beans? Walk on over and say, "Pretty please?"

The silver man leaned forward, examining a readout in the center of the console. He was at the foot of the middle chair.

Lynx, pondering his options, abruptly perceived a risky gambit, a way of giving himself the advantage, and he uttered a trilling sound deep in his throat as he launched his diminutive body forward, bounding across the cockpit. He reached the back of the middle chair in two leaps, his claws digging into the top of the chair as he vaulted upward, his sinewy arms coiling and surging his body up and over the chair. He came over the top like a furry arrow, his fingers extended, his tapered claws grasping for his prey.

The silver man heard a soft noise behind him and started to straighten and turn. He was not anticipating an attack, and he moved slowly.

Which suited Lynx's plans perfectly. He reached the giant just as the silver man completed turning, and his nails ripped into the blond man's uniform at the crotch, shredding the material like so much paper, tearing the silver fabric in a single swift swipe, then spearing inward, aiming at the giant's privates. Lynx intended to slice the blond man's gonads from his body.

But there weren't any.

Lynx's mouth dropped in astonishment as his raking claws closed on empty space where the penis *should* have been. His feet alighted on the chair, and he crouched, preparing to pounce on the silver man's face.

Only the giant was faster. The blond man's initial surprise was fleeting. He twisted to the right as the cat-man tore open his pants, and he swung the clipboard in a brutal arc, backhanding his assailant across the mouth.

Lynx, about to spring, felt the clipboard smash into his lips and teeth. Blood spurted from his mouth as he was knocked onto his back, onto the chair, dazed and vulnerable.

The silver man, the clipboard clutched in his left hand, reached down with his right and clamped his hand on the cat-man's neck. "What have we here?" he asked. "How did you escape your cage?"

Lynx thrashed and pounded at the hand restraining him, to no avail.

"You are wasting your energy," the giant informed the cat-man. "There is no sense in resisting."

Lynx attempted to bite the hand on his neck.

"Feisty mutant, aren't you?" the giant queried.

Lynx pulled out all the stops. He raked his claws along the silver man's right arm, from elbow to wrist, his nails gouging inch-deep furrows in the flesh. A colorless liquid sprayed from the arm, spattering his face. Lynx snarled.

"Cease this foolish resistance this second!" the giant ordered. He raised his left hand above his head, the clipboard poised for another strike.

It never landed.

Ferret flashed from nowhere, his bony fingers rigid, and plunged his fingernails into the giant's eyes, ramming them in and squeezing.

The silver man stiffened, releasing his hold on Lynx, and grabbed at his eyes.

Ferret was clinging to the giant's face, his knees on the blond man's massive chest.

Lynx came up off the chair in a rush, enraged, forgetting his goal, forgetting about Blade and Hickok, thirsting to exact his retribution on the giant. He sprang at the silver man's stomach, his arms slashing in vicious blow after blow, his razor claws rending the silver material and splitting the blond man's abdomen wide open, disgorging a flood of liquid and internal organs. In his rabid frenzy, Lynx concentrated on his attack to the exclusion of all else. His arms flailed again and again, turning the giant's stomach into a stringy, pulpy mess.

"Stop it!" someone yelled.

Lynx grasped a loop of intestine and wrenched the strangely rigid tube from the giant's abdomen.

"Damnit! Stop, Lynx! He's finished!"

Lynx paused, his claws imbedded in the silver man's abdomen. He suddenly realized Ferret was to his left, Gremlin to his right.

"He's finished!" Ferret repeated.

Lynx glanced up.

The giant had slumped backwards against the computer. His torso was inclined at an angle over the console, his hands gripping the computer for support. His legs dangled limply below the ravaged vestige of his waist. Clear fluid seeped from his torn eyes. The left pupil was crushed, but the right was intact, and the right eye gazed at Lynx in bemused amazement.

"Why'd you jump him?" Ferret asked Lynx. "What the hell were you trying to do?"

Lynx stared at the gore coating his nails and hands. "Tryin' to capture him," he mumbled in response.

"Why should you want to do that?" the giant queried in a low tone.

Lynx looked at the silver man. "You can talk?"

"Obviously," the giant replied. "My locomotion is severely impaired, but my vocal apparatus is functional."

"You're lucky it was Ferret here who went for your eyes," Lynx commented. "He ain't got sharp nails like me. I would've ripped your peepers to pieces."

"I believe you," the giant said.

"What do we do now, yes?" Gremlin interjected.

Lynx abruptly realized he was standing on the bottom of the contour chair. He hopped to the floor and peered at the silver man, at the hole in his silver pants. "What are you?" he demanded.

"Beg pardon?" the giant said.

"Don't play games with me, bub!" Lynx stated. "I want to know what you are! Now!"

"I am a Superior," the giant informed them.

"Superior?" Lynx snorted. "Superior to what?"

"To all lower organisms, of course," the Superior answered.

"What lower organisms?" Lynx pressed him.

"Biological organisms," the Superior said.

"Uh-huh." Lynx pursed his lips, his green eyes narrowing. "You ain't told me much. What's a Superior?"

"I am a Superior," the giant reiterated.

"We're talkin' in circles!" Lynx snapped. He reflected for a moment. "Where's your nuts?"

"Beg pardon?" the Superior responded.

Lynx leaned forward, frowning. "I want to know why you ain't got no nuts, pal! No balls! No gonads! Get me?"

The blond man nodded. "Superiors do not require procreational capability."

Lynx and Ferret exchanged glances. "Why not?" Lynx questioned the giant. "Don't you Superior types whoopee?"

"Beg pardon?"

Lynx raised his right hand. "You say that one more time, and I'm gonna finish the job I started! I want to know why you haven't got a pecker, and I want to know now!"

The giant's eyelids fluttered. "Peckers . . . are superfluous."

"They're what?" Lynx said.

"Not essential," the Superior stated wearily.

"What's the matter with you?" Lynx asked. "Are you dyin'?"

"Excessive dehydration," the Superior stated. "My fluid level is critical. You severed one of the major arteries from my Heinlein."

"Your what?" Lynx said.

The Superior's chin dropped onto his chest.

"Don't pass out on me, turkey!" Lynx declared.

The giant's eyes closed, then partially opened. "Unable to maintain sentience," he stated.

Lynx grabbed the silver man's right leg and shook it. "Don't crap out yet! You need to tell me where Blade and Hickok are being held? What happened to 'em?"

The Superior was on the verge of collapsing. "You want the two Warriors?"

"You bet your ass we do!" Lynx asserted. "Where are they? Do you know?"

The Superior nodded. "Containment Section."

"Containment? Where is it?" Lynx probed.

"Sublevels below Intelligence," the Superior revealed, then slumped into unconsciousness, his huge form slipping toward the floor.

Lynx stepped aside as the giant slid from the console and sprawled forward. The silver man's forehead rested on the foot of the center contour chair. "At least he told us a little," Lynx commented.

"He did?" Ferret said. "How do you know we can trust what he said? How do you know he wasn't lying through his teeth?"

Lynx shrugged. "Just a hunch, is all. I think we can believe him. These bozos don't impress me as the lyin' kind."

Ferret smirked. "Is that your professional assessment?"

"Call it whatever you want," Lynx said. "We've got to find this Containment Section and free Blade and Hickok."

"What about this Superior, yes?" Gremlin queried.

"We'll stuff him in one of the closets," Lynx said.

"And what if he's missed?" Ferret asked. "What if someone comes looking for him and finds him?"

"We'll cross that bridge when we come to it," Lynx said. "We haven't got any choice. We can't stay here."

Gremlin stared at the Superior's crotch. "He really does not have a penis, no?"

"No," Lynx confirmed.

"Most unusual, yes?" Gremlin mentioned.

"It's friggin' weird," Lynx remarked. "Come on. Give me a hand."

Together, the three mutants moved the Superior to one of the cockpit compartments and crammed his bulk inside. Lynx propped the Superior against the rear wall, bending the giant's legs perpendicular to the torso.

"There! That should do it!" Lynx said. He closed the compartment door and led the way toward the exit hatch.

"How are we going to find the Containment Section?" Ferret

wanted to know.

"We'll find it," Lynx vowed. "Trust me."

"I wish you'd quit saying that," Ferret muttered.

They were a yard from the exit door when Lynx abruptly halted, his features rippling in surprise.

"What is wrong, yes?" Gremlin asked.

"Those Superiors . . ." Lynx said slowly, his brow creasing in perplexity.

"What about them?" Ferret responded.

"They ain't go no peckers," Lynx stated.

"Yeah. So?" Ferret said.

Lynx glanced at his companions. "So how the hell do they take a leak?"

# 6

Blade came awake with a painful start, his head throbbing, his eyes smarting as a bright light caused him to squint. He remembered the three silver men, and he surveyed his surroundings uncertainly, a dozen questions flooding his mind. What had happened? Where was he? Why had the three silver men jumped him? What was this all about? And, most importantly, why couldn't he move?

A muted humming became audible.

Blade found himself in a square room, ten feet by ten feet. He was the only occupant. The walls, ceiling, and floor were composed of a white, plastic-like substance. A large rectangular light overhead supplied ample illumination. The room was devoid of furniture.

What was going on?

Blade, to his astonishment, discovered he was erect, on his feet in the middle of the room, fully clothed except for his Bowies. His muscular arms were draped at his sides. He tried moving his hands, but failed. Next he attempted to shuffle his legs, but they refused to respond. To his chagrin, he realized his entire body was immobile, with the notable exclusion of his eyes. By focusing all of his attention, he could shift his eyes up and down, and from one side to the other. But the range of movement was slight, compounding his budding frustration.

Had the silver men drugged him?

Blade peered to the right, then the left. The humming seemed to be coming from the walls, emanating from black bubbles positioned in the middle of the white wall to his right and the wall to his left.

What purpose did those black bubbles serve?

Blade was at a loss to explain his predicament. The identity of the silver men was a complete mystery. Why had they abducted him? he wondered. Did they pose a threat to the Home, to the Family? His speculation was unexpectedly terminated as an entrance panel in front of him opened with a dinstinct hiss, gliding to the left.

A woman stood framed in the doorway. A most remarkable woman. She wore a blue dress, the garment scarcely covering her protruding cleavage and exposing her shapely legs up to her thighs. Her narrow lavender eyes glared at him. She had yellow, scaly skin, and long black hair.

Blade endeavored to speak, to move his lips, to address her, but his mouth wouldn't budge.

The woman noticed his effort. She smiled, a particularly wicked expression, and advanced several paces into the room. "The mighty Blade!" she taunted him. "And he can't even talk!"

Blade studied the woman, striving to place her, but he knew he'd never laid eyes on her before in his life.

"Do you know how long I've waited for this moment?" the woman demanded.

Blade could only stare.

The woman glanced at the black bubbles, then at the towering, brooding man. "How does it feel to be helpless? You don't like it, do you? The great Warrior! And you can't even lift your little finger!" She threw back her head and laughed.

Blade waited for the woman to continue.

"Don't you know me?" the woman asked.

Blade's gaze probed her from head to toe.

"I can see you don't," the woman stated. "But then, why should you? We've never met. But I know who you are. I know all about you, you son of a bitch!" Her features twisted, became hateful. "I know you killed the man I loved! I know you for the bastard you are, Blade! So it's only fair you know who I am." She paused, straightened proudly. "I'm Clarissa!"

Blade suddenly recalled one of the silver men mentioning that name, but it didn't ring a bell.

Clarissa took another step toward him, but she was careful not to get too close. "Clarissa! My name might not mean anything to you, you prick! But I know a name that will. The Doktor!''

Blade's eyes widened. The Doktor? The nefarious scientist responsible for countless atrocities? For killing innocent children to further his longevity? For slaughtering thousands, perhaps millions? The demented fiend who'd tried to eradicate the Family? Who'd created genetic deviates to do his bidding, to slay on command?

"You remember the Doktor!" Clarissa said bitterly. "The gentlest man who ever walked this earth! The man whose intellect eclipsed all others! The man who wanted to improve this world, who devoted his genius to establishing order and peace! You remember him, because you're the one who killed him!" Clarissa's voice rose, her tone trembling from her violent emotions. She shook her right fist at the Warrior. "You killed the only man I ever loved! The best man who ever lived! And you're going to pay for what you did!" she gloated.

Insight dawned. Blade scrutinized the woman's face, detecting a hint of madness, and perceived she was responsible for his capture.

"I'm the one who had you brought here!" Clarissa boasted, confirming his suspicion. "I convinced Primator it was necessary!"

Primator? Who—or what—was this Primator?

"But I never expected to get a bonus!" Clarissa went on. "Hickok's death will be an added treat."

Hickok? Blade futilely attempted to raise his arms. What was that about Hickok?

"Hickok tried to save you," Clarissa commented. "But he was caught, just like you. He's in the next room." She jerked her left hand to the left. "You'll go up before Primator together. Don't worry, though. You two will have company. *I'll* be there!" She tittered.

Blade's mind was in turmoil. The news of Hickok's capture was profoundly disturbing.

Clarissa turned to depart, then hesitated. "I'd imagine you have a lot of questions," she said mockingly. "Where you are, for instance? And what's in store for you? Am I right?" She chuckled. "Of course I'm right." She moved to the doorway. "But I'm not about to tell you. I want you to be surprised. I want to see your face when Primator announces your fate."

Blade wished he could reach out and knock her senseless.

"You may be lucky," Clarissa said over her right shoulder. "Primator may relegate you to Servile status. You might be neutered, but at least you'd be alive." She winked, then walked off laughing.

The door hissed shut.

Blade was left with his thoughts and the continuous humming of the black bubbles.

# 7

"Where are we, yes?" Gremlin asked in awe, gaping at the sight before them.

"It certainly isn't Oz," Ferret mentioned.

"Oz?" Lynx repeated.

"A fictional land I read about in one of the books in the Family library," Ferret disclosed. "You should read the book sometime. I think you'd like it."

"What's it about?" Lynx inquired.

"It's about this girl and her dog," Ferret revealed. "They are transported by a tornado to the mystical land of Oz, where they encounter witches and munchkins and wizards and magical slippers."

"Magical slippers?" Lynx reiterated.

"And a tin man, a talking scarecrow, and a cowardly lion," Ferret explained.

"A cowardly lion?" Lynx said skeptically.

"Yeah. It was a terrific book," Ferret said. "You really should read it."

"Weren't you the one who said I should read that other book, the one about Flopsy, Mopsy, and Cottontail?" Lynx inquired.

"I figured you might learn something from it," Ferret commented.

"I did," Lynx said.

"Oh? What?" Ferret responded.

"Never, ever to read another book you recommend," Lynx stated.

"Please!" Gremlin interrupted. "Forget about your books, yes? There are more important matters, no? Like, where are we,

yes?'' He waved his right arm to encompass the panorama surrounding them.

They were outside the huge hangar. They'd waited inside the
aircraft until the coast was clear, then darted behind a nearby
stack of crates. From there, they'd dashed through a side door
onto a loading dock covered with more crates and boxes. Now, as
they crouched in concealment in back of a pile of boxes, they
gazed at the city lights stretching to the far horizon in rapt
fascination.

"It sure ain't Denver," Lynx deduced. "There are too many
lights, too many big buildings. And they all look so new!" he
marveled.

"Look at all the skyscrapers!" Ferret declared.

"Maybe we're in Chicago," Lynx proposed. "Blade told us
about the people there, the Technics. They're supposed to have a
real advanced city."

"This doesn't look like Blade's description of Chicago," Ferret
said, disagreeing. "And Blade didn't see any of those Superior
types in Chicago."

Gremlin was deliberating on the immensity of the city. "How
will we find Blade and Hickok out there, yes? The city is too
large, no?"

"We'll find 'em," Lynx promised.

"Look!" Ferret whispered, pointing.

The north end of the loading dock terminated in a sloping
ramp, and the ramp was a mere ten feet from their hiding place.
Approaching from the base of the ramp was a man in orange
overalls and an orange cap.

"He's normal-sized!" Ferret said. "He must be human."

"Look at that funny doodad on his forehead," Lynx stated.

The loading dock and the ramp were illuminated by lamps
affixed to the hangar walls at 30-foot intervals. In the center of
the advancing man's forehead, clearly visible, reflecting the light,
was a glistening silver circle.

"What do we do, yes?" Gremlin queried anxiously.

Lynx motioned for them to drop from sight. "Leave it to me,"
he advised.

They heard the man's footsteps as he reached the top of the
loading dock, then paused. "Now where's that damn consign-
ment?" the man mumbled.

Lynx cautiously eased his head above the nearest box.

The man in orange was eight feet away, examining the crates and boxes, idly scratching his pointed chin.

Lynx scanned the ramp to insure the man was alone. No one else was in sight.

"Ahhhh! There!" The man exclaimed, and walked toward some crates to his right.

Lynx vaulted over the box screening him, his padded feet landing noiselessly on the cement dock. He took three supple strides and sprang, his arms encircling the man's ankles, his momentum bearing the startled human to the cement.

"What the hell!" the man in orange blurted, and suddenly steely fingers were fastened to his throat, and a pair of feral green orbs blazed into his own brown eyes.

"Don't move, bub!" Lynx threatened. "Or I'll tear your neck open!"

The man in orange froze, petrified.

Ferret and Gremlin quickly raced to join Lynx.

"Give me a hand," Lynx directed, and the trio lifted the human and carted him to their hiding place.

The man in orange gawked as they deposited him on the cement, prone on his back, the cat-man still gripping his throat.

Lynx leaned forward until his nose was almost touching the human's. "I'm gonna let go. But you'd better not squawk, if you know what's good for you! Do you understand?"

The man in orange nodded. He sported a mustache and shallow cheeks.

Lynx released his hold, then knelt on the man's chest. "What's your name?" he demanded.

"Barney," the man blurted out, panic-stricken. "Barney 137496."

"137496?" Lynx said. "What's that?"

Barney seemed confused by the question. "How do you mean?" he replied nervously.

"What's the number for? I asked your name," Lynx stated.

"But that is my name!" Barney stressed. "Barney 137496."

"Your last name is a number?" Lynx queried.

"Of course," Barney answered, bewildered. "Every Servile has an I.D. number."

"Servile? What's a Servile?" Lynx interrogated the human.

Barney was obviously flabbergasted by the cat-man's ignorance. "You don't know what a Servile is? Where are you from?"

Lynx's tone hardened. "I'll ask the questions, pal. What's a Servile?"

"All the workers are Serviles," Barney replied. "All the human workers, that is."

"What other kind of workers are there around here?" Lynx asked.

"There are mutants, like you guys, and . . ." Barney began, then stopped as the cat-man voiced a trilling sound.

"Mutants like us?" Lynx said. "There are mutants here like us?"

"Sure," Barney declared. "Lots of them. But they're in a class all by themselves. They're never called Serviles."

Lynx glanced at Ferret and Gremlin. If there were other mutants in this strange city, where had they come from? The mutations prevalent since World War III were derived from three sources. The first type, the wild mutations found everywhere, were deformed creatures produced by the saturation of the environment with incredible amounts of gene-altering radiation. The second sort, labeled mutates by the Family, were former mammals, reptiles, or amphibians, transformed into pus-covered monstrosities by the chemical toxins unleashed during the war and still prevalent in the environmental chain. And the third form, of which Lynx, Ferret and Gremlin were prime examples, had been deliberately developed in the laboratory by the scientists like the Doktor, genetic engineers intent on propagating new species. But so far as Lynx knew, all of the Doktor's genetic creations had perished. If there were indeed mutants in this city, how had they been produced? Lynx looked at Barney. "What do you call these mutants?"

Barney did a double take. "Mutants," he said.

Ferret snickered.

"Where do the mutants come from?" Lynx inquired.

"From the D.G. Section," Barney revealed.

"What's the D.G. Section?" Lynx wanted to know.

"Deviate Generation Section," Barney elaborated. "Over in Science."

Lynx reflected for a moment. He reached out and tapped the

silver circle in the middle of Barney's forehead. "What do you call this gizmo?"

"It's my O.D.," Barney said.

"O.D.?" Lynx repeated quizzically.

"Orwell Disk," Barney told them.

"What's it for?" Lynx queried.

"Every Servile has one," Barney elucidated. "The mutants too. The Superiors use them to keep tabs on us. They can monitor our activities with them."

Lynx straightened, frowning. He recalled the collars the Doktor had utilized to keep his Genetic Research Division in line. Every mutant the Doktor had developed in his lab had been required to wear the metal collars, collars containing sophisticated electronic circuitry enabling the Doktor to instantly know the location of his test-tube creatures, and to eavesdrop on their conversations. "Can the Superiors hear what you're sayin' with that Orwell Disk?" he asked Barney.

Barney shook his head. "No. They can tell where we are, though, and they know right away if we've strayed into an unauthorized area or are trying to escape Androxia."

"Androxia? Is that the name of this city?" Lynx questioned.

"Sure is," Barney confirmed.

"Where is Androxia?" Lynx queried.

"Where?" Barney said, puzzled.

"Yeah. Where? What state is it in?" Lynx asked.

"Oh. You mean like the old-time states they had before the war?" Barney asked.

"Yep. What state is this?" Lynx said, prompting him.

"It's Androxia," Barney responded. "It's been called Androxia for almost a hundred years, I think."

"But you just said this city is called Androxia," Lynx observed.

"City. State. They're both the same," Barney said.

"You mentioned the old-time states," Lynx stated. "Do you know what this city was before it became known as Androxia?"

Barney pursed his lips. "An old man did tell me a story once, but I don't know how true it is. He said this was once the city of Houston, in a state called Texas. But he was drunk when he told me. Maybe he made the whole thing up."

"Have you ever been outside of Androxia?" Ferret interjected.

"Nope," Barney said. "I was born here. I've always been here. The Superiors don't permit us to leave Androxia."

"And haven't the Superiors ever mentioned anything about Androxia's history?" Ferret inquired.

"No," Barney answered. "Why should they?"

Lynx gazed at the city lights. "Do you know where the Containment Section is located?"

Barney nodded. "In the Intelligence Building. In the lower levels."

"Is it far from here?" Lynx queried.

Barney pointed toward a skyscraper to the northwest. "That's it right there."

Lynx calculated the distance. Not more than a mile, by his reckoning. "Good. Get up. You're gonna take us there."

Barney slowly stood, his frightened brown eyes expanding in alarm. "I can't!" he objected.

"Want to bet?" Lynx countered. He flicked his right arm up, his claws grabbing Barney's coveralls.

"Believe me!" Barney whined. "You don't want me to take you there!"

"Yes we do," Lynx retorted. "We need to get there as fast as possible, and you're our ticket. If you're a good little boy, I'll even let you live, sucker. But we're going, and we're going now, before you're missed."

Barney blanched. "You don't leave me much choice. Just remember I tried to talk you out of it."

Lynx shoved Barney toward the north end of the loading dock. "Lead the way, chuckles! And no tricks, hear?"

Lynx, Gremlin, and Ferret stayed on Barney's heels.

"What if we're spotted, yes?" Gremlin asked.

"So what?" Lynx said. "This wimp says there are mutants like us all over the place. No one will pay any attention to three more."

"I hope *you* know what *we're* doing," Ferret mumbled.

"Trust me," Lynx stated.

Ferret groaned.

The Servile hastily crossed the lot. They passed over a dozen parked vehicles.

Lynx studied the vehicles, impressed. He'd seen scores of conventional cars, trucks, and jeeps in Denver and elsewhere.

They were completely different from the vehicles in the lot. The Androxian conveyances were sleeker, slimmer, with smaller tires and low-slung carriages. They reminded him of rockets on wheels.

"That's Blish Avenue ahead," Barney said, indicating a thoroughfare on the north side of the lot.

Lynx could see sparse traffic flowing on the avenue. "How do we get across it?"

Barney used his left hand and pointed at the northwest corner of the lot. "We can cross there, once the light is green."

The quartet hurried to the northwest corner of the parking lot. They reached a sidewalk bordering Blish Avenue, and 15 yards to the west was an intersection with traffic signals.

"That's Serling Boulevard," Barney said. "We can take it to Intelligence."

"Then let's go," Lynx urged him.

Barney walked to the intersection, then patiently waited for the light to change.

An Androxian car came through the intersection, its motor purring. The interior of the vehicle was lit by a pale blue glow. Behind the steering wheel was one of the silver giants. The Superior glanced at the four figures on the sidewalk, displaying no interest in their presence, and kept going east on Blish Avenue.

"See?" Lynx gloated. "I told you we wouldn't have any trouble."

"We're not there yet," Ferret noted.

"Worrywart," Lynx rejoined.

The traffic signal suspended above the center of the intersection changed from red to green.

"We can cross," Barney said, and started to do so.

Lynx walked to Barney's left, his green eyes scanning Serling Boulevard. The sidewalks contained few pedestrians. "Where is everybody?" he inquired as they reached the far side of the intersection and proceeded north on Serling.

"It's night," Barney replied. "Serviles aren't allowed out at night unless they have a pass, or they're on the night shift. Same with the mutants."

"What is the population of Androxia?" Ferret asked.

"Three million, I think," Barney said. "At least, that's what I heard."

"How many Serviles are there?" Ferret questioned him.

"I don't know," Barney admitted.

"What about the Superiors?" Lynx chimed in. "How many of them are in Androxia?"

"I don't know," Barney said. "They don't tell us stuff like that."

"They don't tell you much, do they?" Lynx remarked.

"They teach us all we need to know," Barney stated.

"Oh? Says who?" Lynx retorted.

"They do," Barney said.

"Real decent of 'em," Lynx cracked sarcastically.

"The Superiors don't mistreat us," Barney mentioned.

"What do you call that Orwell Disk?" Lynx countered.

"Everyone has one," Barney said. "It's no big deal."

Lynx glanced at Ferret. "Nice bunch of sheep they're raisin' here, huh?"

Barney looked at Lynx. "I don't understand. Why are you so hostile towards the Superiors?"

"I don't understand why you're not," Lynx declared.

Barney shrugged. "They provide us with our homes, our clothes, even our food. They don't beat us or anything like that. And they even allow some of us to breed."

"Breed?" Lynx snorted. "You mean they let you poke your squeeze now and then?"

"Squeeze? I don't understand," Barney said.

"You have a wife, dimples?" Lynx asked.

Barney smiled. "Yes. She was my reward for ten years of faithful service to Androxia. We might be permitted to have a child next year. We can hardly wait."

"The Superiors must give the okay for you to have a kid?" Lynx queried.

"Androxia has a population problem," Barney responded. "We must regulate our population numbers."

"You mean the Superiors must regulate the Serviles," Lynx said.

"The Superiors only want what's best for us," Barney said. "What is best for all Androxia."

"Now I know why your eyes are brown," Lynx quipped.

They covered a quarter of a mile in silence, drawing ever closer to the Intelligence Building. A few vehicles passed on Serling Boulevard.

"Barney, what kind of work do you do, yes?" Gremlin inquired at one point.

"I'm night foreman at the Herbert Hangar loading dock," Barney answered.

"You like your job, yes?" Gremlin queried.

"Yeah. I like it a lot," Barney said. "There are a lot worse."

"What kind of work do the mutants around here do?" Lynx questioned.

"Whatever they're bred for," Barney said.

"Bred?" Lynx repeated.

"Yeah. The mutants are assigned to whatever type of work they're bred for. Some are manual laborers. Some work in the Science Section. Others do other jobs," Barney stated.

"Tell me," Lynx said. "Who breeds your mutants?"

"The Superiors, of course," Barney revealed.

"Of course," Lynx said dryly.

"I'd like to know something," Ferret mentioned. "Do the Superiors allow the Serviles to attend school? Did you receive an education?"

"I sure did," Barney said proudly. "I went through all six grades. That's standard. Some, like courier pilots, go longer."

"Six grades? That's all?" Ferret asked.

"Who wants more?" Barney replied. "They teach us to read and write, and math, and whatever other skills we need for our jobs."

"No history, or geography, or any courses like that?" Ferret probed.

"Who needs those?" Barney responded. "The Superiors teach us all we need to know."

"They sure don't teach you to think," Lynx muttered.

"Think? The Superiors take care of all the thinking," Barney said. "They're smarter than us. They know what's best for us."

"So you keep sayin'," Lynx stated.

"Do all of the Serviles feel the same way you do?" Ferret inquired.

"Sure," Barney said, then corrected himself. "Well, not all of them. There are a few who like to cause trouble. They're called

Malcontents.''

"What happens to them?" Ferret asked.

"The Superiors don't allow troublemakers to disrupt anything," Barney said. "The Malcontents are usually sent to the Science Section. When they come out, they're ready to accept their status, to work for the good of all Androxia."

"Why? What happens to 'em in the Science Section?" Lynx queried. "Are they tortured?"

Barney laughed. "No. Of course not! They undergo a simple operation."

"What type of operation?" Ferret said.

"An operation on their brain," Barney said. "To remove the bad cells, I've heard. I think they call it a partial lobotomy."

"A lobotomy, no!" Gremlin declared, aghast. He vividly remembered the experimental lobotomies the Doktor had performed on him, resulting in his aberrant style of speech.

"They're no big deal," Barney said. "Lots of people have them."

"Not just the Malcontents?" Ferret asked.

"No. The mutants, in particular, are operated on a lot. But it's for their own good. The Superiors are only doing what's best for us."

"Do you lick their boots for 'em?" Lynx said sarcastically.

"No," Barney replied. "Why would I want to do that?"

Lynx motioned at Ferret, and they dropped several paces behind Barney and Gremlin.

"What do you make of this garbage?" Lynx inquired.

"The Superiors, whatever they are, totally control the human population here," Ferret stated. "The humans are given a minimal education, just enough to enable them to properly complete their assigned work, and are duped into believing their lives are terrific. Perhaps some form of brainwashing is involved, some psychological techniques we've never heard about. The humans seem to possess no freedom whatsoever, and if Barney is any example, they don't seem to mind."

"Barney is an idiot," Lynx commented.

"But a content idiot," Ferret noted.

"I guess if you don't know you're an idiot," Lynx reasoned, "then you never realize there's more to life than your own stupidity."

Ferret grinned. "Why, Lynx! I'm impressed! That was almost profound. I didn't think you had it in you!" he joked.

"Barney ain't the only dummy around here," Lynx retorted.

The Intelligence Building loomed directly ahead, to the right of the sidewalk. It was an imposing edifice, 40 stories in height, its sides constructed of an opalescent synthetic substance.

Ferret scrutinized their destination. "How are we going to get inside? There are bound to be guards."

"I'll think of something," Lynx asserted.

A small park, consisting of little more than a narrow strip of grass and a row of deciduous trees, separated the sidewalk from the Intelligence Building. As they neared the park, Lynx caught up with the man in orange.

"You've done real fine so far," Lynx said to Barney. "But your job ain't over yet."

Barney slowed. "What do you mean? You wanted me to bring you to Intelligence, and we're almost there. My job is done. Let me go back to the loading dock. Please."

A large vehicle was coming their way, bearing south on Serling Boulevard, its headlights resembling the baleful glare of a gigantic, prowling creature.

"You ain't going back to the dock," Lynx said.

"Please!" Barney pleaded. "Let me return to my work."

"Not on your life," Lynx stated.

The large vehicle, evidently a truck, was 50 yards to the north on Serling.

"If I let you go," Lynx said, "I know you'll run to the Superiors and rat on us."

"I won't!" Barney averred. "I promise!"

The truck was 40 yards away.

"Do you expect me to trust you?" Lynx demanded, grinning. "How dumb do you think I am?"

"I can answer that one," Ferret volunteered.

The truck was 30 yards off.

"Don't bother," Lynx said to Ferret.

Barney glanced at the approaching truck. The corners of his mouth twisted upward. "Don't ever say I didn't warn you," he mentioned. "I tried to tell you. You shouldn't have brought me along."

"You got us here, didn't you?" Lynx stated.

"You made a big mistake," Barney declared.

"Oh?" Lynx responded smugly. "How so?"

At 20 yards' distance, the truck began to slow.

"You remember me telling you about my Orwell Disk?" Barney asked.

"Yeah. So what?" Lynx said.

"I told you the Superiors use the disks to monitor us," Barney remarked.

"So?" Lynx snapped. "If they're millions of you dorks livin' in Androxia, there's no way the Superiors can keep tabs on everybody at once."

"That's where you're wrong," Barney said. "They use computers, and the computers can keep tabs on everyone. Every single one of us. And the minute one of us strays, the minute one of us enters an area we're not supposed to be in, the computer alerts the Superiors."

At ten yards, the truck started to drift across the boulevard.

"Lynx!" Gremlin yelled.

Lynx spun, realizing their peril too late.

The truck angled across the highway, its headlights focusing on the four figures on the sidewalk. Its brakes screeched as it lurched to a halt. The cab was plunged in darkness. The rear consisted of a long, canopy-covered bed. As the truck stopped, its occupants began piling from the back, their black boots smacking on the asphalt as they jumped from the bed. They raced around the cab, converging on the quartet on the sidewalk, fanning out, encircling them.

Barney was smiling triumphantly.

Lynx turned from right to left, debating whether to make a run for it, seeking a way out. But they were surrounded within seconds, hemmed in by a ring of humans and mutants wearing black uniforms and wielding steel batons. There were 12 of them, each one conveying an air of wickedness, each one with a hard, cold expression. Whether human or mutant, neither betrayed the slightest hint of emotion in their eyes. Their black uniforms fit snugly, and their pants were tucked into their black boots. The mutants resembled those in the infamous Doktor's Genetic Research Division, displaying a variety of animalistic traits. Some were decidedly reptilian, others mammalian. Lynx glared at a tall, frog-like form six feet away. He raised his hands and clicked his tapered nails. "Come and get it, sucker! I'm in the mood for frog legs!"

The frog-man didn't respond.

There was a loud click, and the door of the cab swung open. A Superior stepped to the ground. His hair was blond, his face pale, and he wore the typical silver uniform. But clasped in his right hand was a not-so-typical weapon, a coiled whip.

"Oh! We are in trouble, yes!" Gremlin moaned.

The Superior strode toward them, stopping a few feet off. He stared at the dockworker. "Barney 137496. You will explain this unauthorized action, please."

Barney walked up to the Superior. "I'm sorry! I really am! I know I left my post without permission. But I didn't have any choice! These three made me bring them here. They said they had to get to the Intelligence Building."

"Did they use violence on you?" the Superior asked.

"Yes," Barney answered. "That one"—and he pointed at Lynx—"threatened my life."

"Blabbermouth," Lynx said.

"Barney is telling the truth then?" the Superior asked, addressing Lynx.

"Barney is a wimp," Lynx replied.

The Superior looked at Barney. "You will return to your post immediately. You will perform your duties as instructed."

Relief washed over Barney's face. "Of course!"

"You may be questioned by Intelligence tomorrow," the Superior stated.

Barney started to turn, then gazed up at the Superior. "This won't go on my record, will it? I mean, my wife and I are up for procreation approval next year. I hope this won't prevent us from being okayed."

"Your file is without blemish," the Superior said. "You have always met your production quotas, and adhered to all directives. You are rated as an AA-1 Citizen. I do not foresee this incident posing a problem. But if it should come to a hearing, I will personally appear and vouch for your integrity."

Barney beamed in appreciation. "Thank you! Thank you, sir!" He jogged south on Serling, returning to work.

"What a moron!" Lynx cracked.

The Superior stared at Lynx. "The three of you will come with us. Resistance will be useless."

Lynx chuckled. "You ain't takin' us without a fight, chuckles!"

The Superior scrutinized Lynx from head to toe. His gaze rested on Lynx's forehead. "Where is your O.D.?"

"Wouldn't you like to know!" Lynx rejoined.

The Superior glanced at Ferret and Gremlin. "None of you have an O.D. implanted in your forehead as required by directive. How is this possible?"

The ring of humans and mutants in black uniforms never uttered a word. They waited, motionless, the truck and street lights gleaming off the silver disks in their foreheads.

"You will voluntarily enter the truck, now, or suffer the consequences," the Superior said to Lynx.

"Give it your best shot, dimwit!" Lynx stated.

The Superior sighed. His right hand flicked downward, and the ten-foot whip uncoiled and dropped to the asphalt.

Lynx's eyes narrowed. There was something funny about that whip. He'd seen whips before, leather affairs with a lash on the tip. But this one was different. It appeared to be metallic, and the handle was exceptionally large, seemed to be plastic, and contained two red buttons.

"You will not comply with my orders?" the Superior demanded.

Lynx snickered. "Shove it up your ass!"

The Superior's right hand lashed out, the whip arcing through the night air, crackling as it swung toward Lynx.

Lynx ducked under the first strike. He felt the whip miss his back by a hairsbreadth, and his fur tingled as the whip passed.

The Superior calmly swung the whip around, over his head, and snapped his right arm forward.

Lynx saw the whip coming and twisted to the right, seeking to evade the blow. His feline reflexes enabled him to avoid the brunt of the stroke, but not all of it. The very tip of the whip brushed against his left shoulder. Lynx expected to feel a mild stinging sensation. Instead, his entire body was lanced by an agonizing spasm as . . . something . . . coursed through him, jolting him to the core. He twitched and staggered to the left.

"Lynx!" Ferret cried.

Lynx saw the Superior aim another swing of the whip in his direction, and he dodged to the left, his legs sluggish.

The whip bit into Lynx's right arm.

Lynx snarled as his diminutive form was speared by another excruciating surge. Whatever it was, the damn thing was devastating! His arms and legs trembled uncontrollably, his torso jerking, as the whip made contact.

"Lynx! No!" Gremlin shouted, taking a step toward him.

Lynx almost fell. His knees wobbled as he doubled over, stunned by the onslaught.

A fourth time the Superior struck, and the whip looped around the cat-man's neck and held fast.

Lynx stiffened as every fiber of his being was racked by an overpowering force, a force capable of knocking him from his feet and slamming him onto his back. His body bounced and flopped. He attempted to collect his wits, to form coherent thoughts, but failed.

The Superior slowly coiled the whip in his right hand.

Ferret ran to Lynx's side. He glared at the Superior. "What'd you do to him, you bastard? You've killed him!"

"Your companion has not been terminated," the Superior said. "My Electro-Prod was set on Stun, not Kill. He will recover in an hour or so."

Lynx was shuddering, his eyelids quivering.

"Now," the Superior stated in a loud voice. "Will you come with us peacefully, or do you desire to share your friend's fate?"

Ferret glanced at Gremlin. He wanted to aid Lynx, but there was nothing he could do. If they resisted, they would be overwhelmed. One of them might be able to escape, but that would mean deserting Lynx. "What do you say?" he asked Gremlin.

Gremlin frowned, his worried eyes on Lynx. "We have no choice, yes?"

"Yes," Ferret confirmed.

Gremlin's shoulders slumped dejectedly.

"We'll go with you peacefully," Ferret told the Superior.

"A logical decision," the Superior said. He waved his left arm, and two of the men in black stepped forward and lifted Lynx in their arms. They carried him toward the rear of the truck.

"You will follow your friend," the Superior directed.

"Where are you taking us?" Ferret inquired as he moved past the silver man.

"You will be taken to Containment and held there until Intelligence interrogates you," the Superior disclosed.

"Did you say Containment?" Ferret asked.

"Yes. Why?" the Superior said.

"Oh, no reason," Ferret declared, then burst out laughing.

The Superior watched, perplexed, as the mutant with the long nose climbed onto the bed of the truck, laughing all the while. The third one, the mutant with the gray skin and red eyes, was grinning. Odd behavior, he mentally observed, considering they were probably Malcontents and would be lobotomized within 24 hours. The lower orders were becoming more bizarre every day.

# 8

The young guard in the black uniform, a tray of food in his hands, entered Stasis Cell 43 and paused, puzzled.

The one in buckskins was still unconscious.

The guard advanced to within four feet of the prisoner. Any closer and the stasis bubbles would effect him. He peered at the captive's face. Why was the man still out like a light? he wondered. The prisoner should have recovered hours ago.

The man in the buckskins was suspended in midair between two of the humming black bubbles. His chin was slumped on his chest.

The guard lowered the tray to the floor. Perhaps the prisoner had sustained an internal injury, he speculated. He knew the captive's file indicated a head blow was the cause of the unconsciousness. Should he call Medical and have them send over a Med-Tech? The guard decided he wouldn't. If he phoned up a Med-Tech, and the prisoner wasn't seriously injured, it would make him look foolish.

So what should he do?

The guard was in a quandary. He was required to feed the prisoner. The usual procedure was to deposit the tray near a captive, then deactivate the stasis field and quickly step back, his hand on his baton, and wait until the meal was consumed. But this prisoner could hardly eat his meal while unconscious.

There was only one feasible recourse.

The guard elected to rouse the captive himself. He walked to the left wall and pressed a black button situated at shoulder height. Immediately, the humming emanating from the stasis bubbles became fainter and fainter, finally ending altogether. As the humming decreased in intensity, the prisoner gradually slumped to the floor. He wound up on his forehead and knees, his arms splayed from his sides.

"Let's have a look at you," the guard remarked, and stepped over to the captive and knelt down. "Why aren't you awake?" he asked, reaching for the prisoner's shoulders.

"Who says I'm not?" the buckskin-clad figure replied, and came up off the floor in a rush, his fists clenched.

Startled, the guard grabbed for the baton in the sheath on his right hip.

The man in the buckskins was faster. His left fist clipped the astonished guard on the jaw, sending him sprawling. The guard tried to scramble erect, but a crushing right fist connected with his left cheek, knocking him to the floor, dazing him.

"Don't move!" the prisoner snapped, yanking the baton from the sheath and raising it over his head. "Don't even twitch, or I'll bash your head in!"

The guard, flat on his back, froze. He'd used the steel baton on numerous occasions and was well aware of the damage one could inflict.

"Where's my hardware?" the prisoner demanded.

"Your what?" the guard said nervously.

"My hardware! My irons! My guns!" the man in buckskins declared angrily.

"I don't know."

The prisoner's mouth curled downward, and he elevated the baton a little higher, his blue eyes on the silver disk in the guard's forehead.

"Honest, I don't!" the guard stated anxiously. "Your weapons were confiscated before they brought you here. We're not allowed to touch a gun. They're illegal in Androxia for anyone except Superiors."

"Damn!" the prisoner snapped in annoyance. "I don't savvy half of what you said. Androxia? Superiors? What are you yappin' about?"

The guard didn't know what to say.

"Where's my pard?" the prisoner inquired angrily.

"Your what?"

"My pard. Blade. He was captured about the same time I was," the man in buckskins said.

The guard suddenly recalled the name on the prisoner's file.

"You're called Hickok, right?"

Hickok leaned forward menacingly. "I know that, horseshit for brains! What I *don't* know is where Blade is! Now where is he?"

The guard gulped, his brown eyes riveted on the baton. "He's in the next cell over. Number forty-four."

"Take me to him!" Hickok directed.

The guard slowly stood. "You won't get away with this," he remarked.

"Did I ask your opinion?" Hickok rejoined.

The youthful guard led Hickok from Stasis Cell 43 and took a left in the corridor outside.

Hickok scanned the corridor. The walls, floor, and ceiling were white, like those in the cell. Square lights recessed in the ceiling lit the hallway, revealing dozens of doors on both sides, each with a red number near the top. No one else was in the corridor. "Where are the other guards?" he asked.

"I'm the only one on duty," the guard replied.

"Don't lie to me!" Hickok warned.

"I'm not lying," the guard insisted. "There's only one guard per block on night shift."

They reached the next door, Number 44.

"This is it," the guard announced.

"Open it," Hickok ordered.

The guard reached to the left of the door, pressing a black button on the wall.

The door to Cell 44 hissed open.

Hickok saw Blade suspended in the cell between two of the black bubbles. He took a step forward, concentrating on his friend.

And the guard struck. He lunged, his arms extended, and he succeeded in wrapping them around the Warrior's waist as the gunman spun to confront him.

Hickok felt the guard's right shoulder drive into his stomach, and he was propelled off his feet and slammed onto his back in the cell, the guard on top of him.

The guard raised up, swinging his right fist at the Warrior's face.

Hickok twisted his head to the left, and the guard's blow glanced off his cheek. Before the guard could regain his balance and punch again, Hickok let him have it with the baton, his right

arm sweeping up and around, smashing the steel baton on the
guard's thin lips, crushing several of his teeth, and causing the
guard to abruptly go limp and slump backwards to the floor,
blood trickling from his mouth.

Hickok quickly rose. "Blasted vermin!" he muttered, and
kicked the guard in the face for good measure. He turned, and
found Blade's eyes on him. "What are you lookin' at?" He
moved to the left wall, searching for a black button similar to the
one the guard had pressed in his cell. The stupid kid had believed
he was unconscious, but he had been playing possum, and he'd
seen everything the guard had done.

Blade's eyes followed the gunman's movements.

Hickok spied the black button. "Have you free in a sec, pard,"
he said, and stabbed the button.

Instantly, the humming tapered off as the black bubbles grew
silent.

Blade's massive body eased to the floor, onto his knees. He
tentatively moved his arms and worked his jaw muscles. "You did
it!" he said after a minute, elated.

"Naturally," Hickok stated. "It was a piece of cake."

Blade slowly stood. "How'd you do it?"

"I'll tell you about it later," Hickok said. "Right now, we'd
best vamoose before more guards show up."

"Do you know where we are?" Blade inquired.

"Nope," Hickok said. "Some kind of prison, it looks like."

Blade walked to the doorway. "Are there any more guards
around here?"

"I don't think so," Hickok said.

"Any idea what they did with our weapons?" Blade queried.

Hickok wagged the baton at the prostrate guard. "That cow
chip told me they were confiscated. I don't know where they
are."

Blade frowned. "Did a woman named Clarissa come to see
you?"

Hickok shook his head. "No. Why? Your missus is going to be
mighty ticked off if she finds out you've been steppin' out on
her."

"Very funny," Blade stated. "Have you ever heard her name
before?"

"Clarissa? It doesn't sound familiar," Hickok mentioned.
"Why? Who is she?"

"She claims to have been in love with the Doktor—" Blade began.

"The Doktor?" Hickok interrupted. "That scum!"

"And she might be the reason we're here," Blade went on.

"How so?" Hickok probed.

"She showed up in my cell," Blade elaborated. "Said something about getting revenge for what I did to the Doktor."

"So that's why those silver varmints came to the Home?" Hickok asked.

"Evidently," Blade said.

"I sure hope I bump into this Clarissa," Hickok remarked. "I want to thank her, personal-like, for all the trouble she's put us through."

"I have the feeling our troubles are just beginning," Blade commented.

"Brother!" Hickok exclaimed in mock indignation. "A few measly clouds appear on your horizon, and you go all to pieces, don't you?"

Blade ignored the barb and stepped into the corridor. "Which way do you think we should go?"

Hickok joined his fellow Warrior. "Makes no never-mind to me, pard. You're the head Warrior. You decide."

"Thanks," Blade said, and moved to the right.

"We've got to find our where the blazes we are," Hickok noted.

"And find a way of returning to the Home," Blade said. "Do you know how they brought us here?"

"Yep. In some fancy flyin' contraption," Hickok disclosed.

"You saw it?"

"Sure did. You were out cold when they brought you on board. I tried to save you, but those silver guys are hard to stop," Hickok said.

"Don't I know it," Blade concurred.

Hickok abruptly halted, his expression betraying shock.

Blade stopped. "What's the matter with you?"

"It just hit me!" Hickok declared. "We'd best check out all of these holding cells."

"Why?"

"Because the runt and his two shadows might be prisoners," Hickok said.

Blade's brow creased in consternation. The gunman used the

term "runt" to describe only one person: Lynx. "Are you telling me that Lynx, Ferret, and Gremlin might be here too?"

"Afraid so," Hickok said.

"What did you do?" Blade asked. "Bring the whole Family along?"

"They snuck on board the aircraft with me," Hickok explained. "I don't know what happened to the dummies. We hid out when the silver yahoos came on the aircraft. I didn't see hide nor hair of 'em after that."

Blade scanned the length of the corridor. "Do you know how long it will take to search every cell?"

"It wasn't my fault," Hickok reiterated.

Blade sighed and moved to the nearest door. "How do we open one of these."

Hickok nodded toward the black button on the wall. "Press that."

Blade did, and the cell door hissed open. The cell was empty. "This will take forever," he remarked.

Hickok glanced to their left, then suddenly grabbed Blade's right wrist and pulled him into the cell.

"What is it?" Blade queried.

"The door at the end of the hall was opening," Hickok said. "I didn't wait to see who it was."

Blade spotted another black button on the interior wall near the door and pressed it. The door closed.

Hickok pressed his ear to the door. "I can hear somebody comin'," he stated.

Blade placed his right ear to the door. He could hear the tread of multiple footsteps in the corridor, increasing in volume as they neared the door. Voices became audible.

" . . . until morning," a deep voice was saying. "I am incapable of fabricating a falsehood. When I told you your friend was not seriously injured, I spoke the truth."

"But he's still shaking, yes?" responded a familiar speaker.

"That's Gremlin!" Hickok whispered.

"His body absorbed an enormous voltage," the first voice stated. "Nervous system and muscular control are directly affected. I told you he would recover in an hour. It has not yet been twenty minutes. When you see him in the morning, he will be fully recovered."

"I hope so," said a third voice.

"That's Ferret!" Hickok said.

Blade knew their voices as well as the gunfighter. He frowned, annoyed. Escape was no longer a simple matter of finding an exit from the prison. Now they would need to rescue the three mutants, then seek an exit—and in the process increase the risk of detection and recapture. But there was no other option. Lynx, Ferret, and Gremlin were adopted Family members. The three mutants had thrown in with the Family and had aided the Warriors on numerous occasions. Abandoning them was out of the question.

"Where is the guard on duty?" asked the deep voice, sounding as if he was right outside the cell door.

Blade tensed. They had left his cell door open after knocking out the guard! If whoever was out in the corridor kept going, they would reach the open cell and discover the unconscious guard!

"You will remain here while I go back to the guard station at the end of the hall and use their phone," the deep voice directed. "I'll patch into the Rice O.D. Locator Computer and have the guard's location pinpointed within seconds."

"Is that how you found Barney so fast?" Ferret asked.

"The computer registered Barney's deviation from his assigned work area the second he departed with you," the deep voice said.

There was the sound of a single person moving away.

Hickok nudged Blade. "Should we try and free 'em?" he whispered.

Blade shook his head. He leaned next to the gunman's left ear. "No. We don't know how many are with them. That one doing all the talking sounded like one of those silver jokers. We'll wait."

Hickok nodded.

More talking arose in the corridor.

"Lynx! Lynx! Snap out of it!" Ferret said.

"He's in bad shape, yes?" Gremlin mentioned.

"I just hope he comes around like that big bastard said he would," Ferret declared.

Silence.

Blade waited, straining for the faintest sound. Finally, the man with the deep voice returned.

"Most peculiar," he stated. "The duty guard is in a cell not far ahead. You four! Check Cell forty-four immediately."

Boots pounded on the floor. Within ten seconds, someone was shouting from the direction of Cell 44. "He's in here, RH-10! He's been attacked!"

"Is he alive?" RH-10 asked.

"Yes, sir! But he's unconscious!"

"Revive him!" RH-10 ordered. His voice lowered. "There must have been an escape. We didn't pass anyone on the west stairwell, so the escapee might be using the east one. You six! Take the east stairwell to the ground floor. Detain anyone not in uniform."

"Yes, sir!" someone responded, and boots tramped off to do his bidding.

"You two will remain here. I must return to the guard station and activate the alarm," RH-10 said. He walked off.

Blade's mind was racing. If he'd understood RH-10's directions, then Hickok and he were in a cell on the north side of the hallway. To the left was east, to the right west. RH-10, obviously one of the silver men, was heading for the west end of the corridor, where the guard station was apparently located. Six other men were on their way to the stairwell at the east end. Four more were in Cell 44. And only two were guarding Lynx and others.

"Should we try and free 'em now?" Hickok questioned softly.

Blade thoughtfully chewed on his lower lip. There were only two avenues of escape from the cell block, the two stairwells. The silver man was at the west end, the six others on the east side. Even if Lynx, Ferret and Gremlin could be freed, how could the five of them manage to use the stairwells unseen? The answer was simple: they couldn't. He glanced at Hickok and shook his head.

Minutes elapsed.

Someone in the corridor coughed.

The next moment the entire corridor was rocked by the blaring wail of klaxons.

Blade's frustration was mounting. They had been so close to freedom! And now they were trapped inside the prison, while their enemies were scouring every nook and cranny to find them. He felt cornered and helpless, and the short hairs on the nape of his neck were tingling.

Out of the frying pan, into the fire!

# 9

Gremlin placed his hands over his sensitive ears and grimaced in discomfort. "The sirens are too loud, yes? They hurt Gremlin's ears!"

Ferret, standing two feet away, supporting Lynx, his left arm draped around Lynx's waist, his right bracing Lynx's chest, nodded.

Two of the men in black were four feet off to the west, their hands on their batons, alertly watching the three mutants.

RH-10 hurried toward them from the guard station at the west end of the corridor. "Security will lock every exit from the building," he announced. "Blade will not escape."

"Blade?" Ferret said in surprise.

"The cell chart indicates Blade was being detained in Cell Forty-four," RH-10 said. "Somehow, he must have neutralized the stasis field. Most exceptional. No one has ever done that before."

"You'll never catch Blade," Ferret said.

"He was captured once," RH-10 noted. "We will apprehend him again."

"Blade doesn't make the same mistake twice," Ferret said, baiting the silver figure.

"We shall see," RH-10 commented. "In the meantime, we must confine the three of you." He lifted his right arm and motioned with his whip at the closed door. "Place the one called Lynx in there," he directed the two men in black.

The pair moved to the front of the cell door. One of them pressed the black button in the wall, and the door slid aside.

For a second, the tableau was frozen, the two men in black

gaping in amazement at the two Warriors in the cell.

Hickok reacted first, charging forward and ramming into one of the men, slamming his foe into the far wall.

Blade surged from the cell, his huge right fist crashing into the other man in black, crushing the hapless man's nose and sending him toppling to the side.

RH-10, five feet away, lunged forward, bringing his right arm up.

Blade saw the peculiar whip in the silver giant's hand, and he wasn't about to give his adversary time to employ the weapon. He took one stride and vaulted into the air, executing a flying kick, his left leg striking the giant's right hand and deflecting the whip, even as he swept his left fist in a vicious arc, his knuckles smashing into RH-10's mouth and pulverizing the giant's lips.

RH-10 tried to step backwards, to give himself more room to bring his whip to bear.

Blade closed in, pressing his advantage. His right moccasin flicked up and out, connecting with RH-10's left kneecap. There was a loud snap, and RH-10 staggered.

So! The bastards weren't invulnerable!

Blade kicked again, going for RH-10's right knee, and something cracked as he landed his blow.

RH-10 tottered, struggling to stay erect.

Blade gripped RH-10's silver collar, and with every muscle on his immensely powerful frame straining to the limit, he lifted the silver giant from the floor, then whipped RH-10 to the right, ramming the silver man's head into the wall.

RH-10 felt some of his fluid splatter over his eyes as his forehead caved in from the brutal impact. He tried to claw at the Warrior's face.

Blade swung the silver giant a second time, pounding RH-10's forehead into the wall again.

RH-10 stiffened. His hands drooped to his sides, and the metallic whip fell to the floor.

Blade shoved the silver giant backwards, releasing his hold.

RH-10 stumbled for a few feet, then attempted to straighten. His legs buckled, and he pitched backwards, crashing onto his broad back.

Blade whirled.

Hickok had already disposed of the other man in black. Ferret was still supporting Lynx, and Gremlin's mouth looked like it wanted to sag to his navel.

"This way!" Blade directed, motioning to the west. "Make for the stairwell."

Ferret started to comply. He paused and nodded at the whip. "You might want to bring that. It may come in handy."

Blade stooped and retrieved the metallic whip. The 15-inch handle felt warm to the touch. He noticed a pair of red buttons, wondering about their purpose.

Hickok hurried past Blade. "I wish we had some iron," he said. "This baton is for sissies."

Gremlin was gawking at the fallen silver giant.

"Move it!" Blade ordered.

Gremlin hastened after Ferret and Hickok. "You did it, yes!" he said to Blade. "You defeated a Superior, yes!"

"A Superior?" Blade repeated quizzically.

"You didn't know, no?" Gremlin said. "They are called Superiors, yes."

"You can tell me about it later," Blade stated. "Catch up with the others."

Ferret, Lynx, and Hickok were already 15 yards away.

Gremlin nodded and jogged to the west.

"Hey! You!" shouted a belligerent voice from the east.

Blade turned.

Five figures in black uniforms were clustered in front of Cell 44. One of them was woozy, leaning against the wall. The other four had drawn their batons.

"Don't move!" one of them, a squat, frog-like mutant with green skin and bulging eyes, yelled.

Blade glanced over his right shoulder. His friends had a long way to go before they reached the door at the west end of the corridor. He had to prevent the men in black from getting past him!

"Don't move!" the frog-man cried, and four of them charged toward the Warrior.

Blade waited for them in the center of the hall. What were they? he speculated. Storm troopers? Security police? He flicked his right wrist, uncoiling the metallic whip to its full ten-foot length.

And a strange thing happened.

The four troopers checked their advance, slowing to a cautious shuffle, their eyes riveted on the metallic whip.

What was this?

Blade glanced at the whip handle. Why would four professional military types be afraid of a mere whip? A whip could lacerate the flesh, might even take out an eye or lash off an ear, but a blow from a whip was rarely fatal. From an ordinary whip, anyway. But what if the whip in his hand *wasn't* ordinary? His thumb closed on the first red button, and the whip abruptly crackled and sparkled, writhing like a thing alive. Now he knew! The whip was electrified!

The four in uniform halted. Twenty feet separated them from the hulking Warrior.

Blade grinned. If the troopers were deathly afraid of the whip, he could use their fear to gain the upper hand. He remembered an ancient axiom: a good offense is always the best defense. With that in mind, he attacked.

The four troopers bumped into one another as they attempted to flee, to avoid the path of the swinging whip.

Blade swung the whip from side to side, from one wall to the other, as he bore down on the four troopers. One of them, the frog-man, tripped and sprawled onto his stomach. Blade slashed the tip of the whip toward the mutant.

The frog-man was almost to his feet when the whip landed between his shoulder blades. There was a brilliant flash, and the frog-man reacted as if he'd been blasted from a canyon. His body soared over eight feet and collided with another of the troopers, knocking the man to the floor. The mutant smacked onto his abdomen, then was motionless.

Blade pressed his initiative, closing in.

The trooper the frog-man had bowled over frantically scrambled erect.

Blade arced the whip in a looping motion, and the metallic lash coiled around the trooper's neck.

The trooper screamed as his body twitched spasmodically. His arms flapped wildly, and he inadvertently touched the steel baton in his right hand against the whip. There was a loud retort, a burst of white light, and the trooper reeled a few feet, then dropped.

Blade paused.

The other two men in black were fleeing for their lives to the east. They passed the trooper leaning against the wall near Cell 44, and he joined their pell-mell flight.

Blade let them go. Chasing them would be a waste of energy. He needed to reach the west stairwell as promptly as he could. The whip emitted a sinister sizzling sound. He pressed the first red button and the sizzling ceased.

"Blade! Come on, pard!" Hickok yelled to his rear.

Blade looked to the west. Hickok, Ferret, Lynx, and Gremlin were standing next to the door at the end of the hallway. He turned to race after them, then hesitated, curious. He quickly knelt alongside the last trooper he'd downed and felt for a pulse.

The trooper was dead.

Blade rose and raced toward his companions. The whip was lethal! Little wonder the four troopers had balked at confronting him. Their steel batons were not very effective against an electrified whip. Why, he asked himself, didn't the troopers pack guns? He thanked the Spirit they didn't! Otherwise, escaping from the prison would be next to impossible.

Hickok was motioning for Blade to hurry.

Blade increased his pace, and reached the door without further mishap.

"Took you long enough," Hickok greeted him. "Maybe you should consider going on a diet."

Blade disregarded the gunfighter and glaced at Ferret. "How's Lynx?"

"Still out of it," Ferret replied. "But he should come around soon."

"Let's hope so," Blade commented, reaching for the door handle.

Gremlin pointed at another door, one to the left marked GUARD STATION 30. "Should we check in there, yes?"

"No," Blade said. "There's no time. The ones who got away will be back with help." He suddenly realized the klaxons weren't wailing anymore. When had they stopped?

"You want me to take the point?" Hickok queried.

"I will," Blade said. "You bring up the rear. And yell if you see any sign of pursuit."

"Wouldn't you prefer a chorus of 'Home on the Range'?" Hickok asked.

"A yell will do," Blade told him, and opened the stairwell

door. The stairs were painted red, and they only went in one direction: up. Which meant, Blade reasoned, they were on the lowerest underground level. He headed up the stairs, two at a stride.

"Slow down!" Ferret said. "I can't keep up with you and carry Lynx at the same time."

Blade slackened his speed. He reached a landing and stopped, waiting for the others to reach him, his eyes on the closed stairwell door.

Ferret, with Gremlin assisting, lugged Lynx onto the landing. "Did you know we're six floors underground?" he asked Blade.

"Are you sure?" Blade responded.

"Positive," Ferret asserted. "I counted them on the way down. Am I right, Gremlin?"

"Ferret is right, yes," Gremlin confirmed.

"They have elevators in this building," Ferret went on. "But near as I could tell, the elevators don't descend below ground level. Must be a security precaution."

Hickok reached the landing. "Leave it to you yokels to take time to gossip when we're close to buyin' the farm."

"Let's keep going," Blade said, resuming his climb. Two more landings were attained without any sign of the enemy. He halted, not wanting to outdistance his friends.

"Lynx is regaining consciousness," Ferret announced when they joined the chief Warrior.

Lynx was moaning, his head lolling, and his mouth was twitching.

"Let me know if he wakes up," Blade directed, continuing his ascent. He kept climbing until he found a door labeled LOBBY.

Ferret and Gremlin, with Lynx held between them, reached the landing seconds later. "Is this the ground floor?" Ferret queried hopefully.

Blade pointed at the door. "I think so."

Hickok dashed up to the landing. "Company is coming," he declared.

Blade crossed to the edge of the landing and peered over the railing.

Black forms were visible at the very bottom of the stairwell, climbing upward.

"We can't wait for Lynx to snap out of it," Blade said to

Ferret. "Gremlin and you will have to carry him. Stay close to Hickok and me. The first exit door we see, we're out of here."

"The Superior said all exits would be locked, yes," Gremlin reminded them.

"What the blazes is a Superior?" Hickok asked.

Blade moved to the stairwell door. "Later. Stick with me and don't be bashful about using that baton."

Hickok grinned. "Since when have I ever been bashful?"

Blade took a deep breath, then opened the lobby door, prepared for the worst. He found it.

The lobby was packed with troopers. Dozens of them, milling about, conversing, evidently awaiting instructions. Directly opposite the stairwell door were six glass doors leading to the outside. A trooper was stationed in front of each one.

Blade frowned. He glanced to the right, spying a row of elevators lining the east wall. To the left was a counter with more troopers behind it, some doing paperwork, others talking.

"Hey! Look!" one of the troopers in the center of the lobby shouted. "The stairwell!"

All eyes swiveled toward the stairwell door.

"Damn!" Blade fumed, and burst from the stairwell, activating the whip. He plunged into the mass of troopers, swinging the whip like a madman, cracking it left and right, sparks flying as the whip crackled and sizzled.

Bedlam ensued. Crammed close together, the troopers were unable to fan out, unable to avoid the terrible whip. Some of them screeched as their bodies were jolted by a blow from the lash. Others endeavored to bring their batons into action, without success.

Blade whirled in one direction, then another, his right arm constantly in motion, knowing he couldn't afford to slacken his pace for an instant. The muscles in his right arm bulged as he flicked the whip every which way. To the right, and he slashed a trooper's neck open and sent the trooper hurtling into those nearby. To the left, and he seared a trooper's eyes as the whip danced across the trooper's face. The trooper was flung backwards, plowing into others, upending them in a tangle of limbs.

The men in black parted, clearing a narrow path in front of the maniac with the whip.

Blade was half the distance to the glass doors when a new threat presented itself.

One of the silver giants appeared, and he was wielding a whip of his own.

Blade saw the silver figure emerge from the pack, and he dodged to the left as the silver giant's whip hissed toward him. The Superior missed by a fraction. Blade brought his whip up and around, charging forward as he did, and a fantastic flash of light seemed to fill the lobby as the silver giant was struck in the chest.

The Superior tottered, shaking his head in a vain attempt to unscramble his thoughts.

Blade let the silver giant have a second taste of the lash.

The Superior was hit on the nose, and his head rocked backwards as his huge bulk was thrown to the floor. He thrashed and bucked, his legs quivering, smoke filtering from his dilated nostrils. His whip clattered from his grasp.

Hickok materialized from nowhere, diving across the floor, sliding up to the quaking silver giant and scooping the Superior's whip from the floor by the handle. He leaped to his feet, stroking the whip at their foes, using the weapon as he'd seen Blade do, beaming. "Come and get it, you mangy coyotes!" he shouted.

Blade reentered the fray, adding his whip to Hickok's.

The troopers wavered, their courage diminished by the defeat of the presumably invincible Superior. As the two Warriors tore into them with renewed fury, the troopers broke, fleeing, some seeking shelter behind the counter, others making for the elevators, still others retreating into the stairwell.

Blade and Hickok abruptly found themselves within ten feet of the glass doors without a trooper to oppose them.

Hickok ran to the doors.

Blade glanced over his right shoulder, finding the three mutants about ten feet to his rear. "Come on!" he urged them, and together they rushed to the gunfighter's side.

"They're locked!" Hickok cried. "The damn doors are locked!"

Blade scanned the lobby. Troopers were still taking cover. The Superior was inert except for his fluttering eyelids. The Superior! Blade darted over to the prone silver giant, deactivated his whip, then gripped the Superior's left boot and dragged the body toward the glass doors.

Hickok was wrenching on one of the doors, trying to force it open.

"Stand back!" Blade cautioned them. He stuck the whip handle under his belt, then grasped the front of the Superior's silver garment and hauled the silver giant into the air. The veins on his temples protruded as he raised the Superior over his head, and his complexion flushed as he took three rapid strides and hurled the silver giant at the third glass door from the left with all of his prodigious might.

The glass doors were not shatterproof. The third one disintegrated in a shower of zinging shards as the Superior's hurtling form crashed into the glass, and the silver giant's body tumbled to the sidewalk beyond amidst the fractured fragments of the glass panel.

Hickok was first through the door, stepping over the Superior's lifeless figure. He assisted Ferret and Gremlin in hefting Lynx over the threshold.

Blade, after a last look to insure none of the troopers were dogging them, exited the building. He surveyed their surroundings, delighted to discover a truck parked not 20 feet away next to the sidewalk. "To the truck!" he commanded, and led off.

Hickok stayed to the rear, covering their escape.

Blade reached the truck cab and yanked open the driver's door. He clambered inside and groped along the steering column.

The keys were there!

Blade jumped to the ground. The truck was a transport of some kind, with a large bed covered by a canvas canopy.

Ferret, Gremlin, and Lynx joined him.

"In the cab!" Blade said. "It'll be a tight squeeze, but all of us should be able to fit."

"What's going on?" Lynx mumbled, his green eyes focusing on Blade, his feline features twisted in bewilderment.

"We'll fill you in as we go along," Blade told him. "Can you move under your own power?"

"Don't think so," Lynx responded. "Legs feel like mush."

Blade jerked his left thumb toward the cab.

Ferret nodded, and with Gremlin's help hoisted Lynx up into the truck cab. They slid across the seat to the far side.

"They're regrouping near the glass doors!" Hickok announced as he caught up with them.

"Into the truck," Blade directed.

Hickok promptly complied, sitting in the middle of the wide seat.

Gremlin was pressed against the far door. Ferret sat between Gremlin and the gunfighter with Lynx in his lap.

Hickok glanced at Ferret and Lynx, grinning. "Don't you two look cozy!" he quipped.

Lynx stared at the Warrior. "When I'm fully recovered," he said slowly, "remind me to rip your face off."

Blade vaulted into the cab, slammed the door, started the engine, and flicked on the headlights. He studied the dashboard, noting it was somewhat similar to vehicles he'd encountered in the Civilized Zone. Like most of them, the truck was an automatic, but it was in brand-new condition, while the majority of the vehicles in the Civilized Zone and elsewhere were holdovers from the prewar civilization and the decade or so following World War III, when a few of the manufacturing facilities were negligibly operational. The prewar society had evinced a marked predilection for automatic transmissions in their vehicles, and very few vehicles with manual transmissions were still on the road. Some of the military vehicles used them, but otherwise automatics were the rule. Blade had driven a truck with a manual transmission in the past, but he preferred an automatic, and he was relieved when he discovered he wouldn't need to contend with shifting gears and using a clutch.

"What are you waitin' for?" Hickok asked. "World War Four?"

Blade put the truck in Drive and accelerated, wheeling the transport along a drive curving toward an avenue beyond a small park.

"That's Serling Boulevard," Ferret stated as the truck neared the thoroughfare.

"How do you know that?" Blade inquired, scanning Serling for other traffic. He saw two cars to the left, heading toward them.

"We were coming to find you when we were caught," Ferret explained. "We were on Serling, right near the dinky park there, when one of those Superiors and his goons showed up in this truck. The damn Superior used his whip on Lynx. They had us climb in the back of the truck, then drove into this driveway."

Blade braked as he came to the end of the driveway. He noticed a red sign to the right. The transport's headlights illuminated the lettering on the sign. It read STOP.

"I'd like to find that son of a bitch with the whip!" Lynx interjected.

"Blade already took care of him," Ferret said.

Lynx gazed at Blade. "Did you waste the sucker?"

"I don't know," Blade said, mentally debating whether to turn right or left on Serling.

"You don't know?" Lynx responded.

"I broke both of his legs and busted his head wide open," Blade elaborated. "But there wasn't time to see if he was still alive."

"Broke his legs and busted his noggin, huh?" Lynx said, and chortled. "That'll teach those dorks to mess with us!"

Blade decided to take a right, away from the approaching cars. He turned the steering wheel, the transport gaining speed.

Lynx was tittering.

"What are you so blamed happy about?" Hickok queried.

"I feel strong again," Lynx said. "I'm back to normal."

"Normal is one thing you're not," Hickok said.

"What's that crack supposed to mean?" Lynx demanded, bristling.

"Oh, nothing," Hickok replied innocently.

"Are you makin' fun of me because I'm a mutant?" Lynx asked angrily.

Hickok stared into Lynx's eyes. "You know I'd never do that, pard. I was just referring to the fact you're a feisty runt with an ego the size of the moon."

Ferret laughed. "Three points for Hickok."

Lynx was about to voice a testy retort, when he abruptly grinned and nodded. "I've always said you have a great sense of humor."

"Since when?" Hickok rejoined.

"Ask anybody," Lynx said.

"Ferret?" Hickok asked.

"I never heard Lynx compliment your sense of humor," Ferret replied.

"Thanks a lot!" Lynx snapped.

"I knew it," Hickok said.

"But I do remember him saying something about you once," Ferret added.

"Oh? What was that?" Hickok inquired.

"Lynx said you were such a hardhead," Ferret stated, grinning, "that you must have granite between your ears."

"Now *that* sounds like Lynx," Hickok said.

"It was a joke!" Lynx exclaimed. "Don't tell me an intelligent, devoted, skilled Warrior like yourself can't take a little joke?"

Hickok gazed at Lynx suspiciously. "Okay. What's with all the praise, runt?"

"I'm just tellin' it like it is," Lynx said.

"What are you up to?" Hickok demanded.

"Not a thing," Lynx replied sweetly.

"Bet me!" Hickok rejoined.

"Is this any way to treat someone who pulled your fat out of the fire?" Lynx asked indignantly.

"What?" Hickok responded in disbelief.

"That's right, chuckles," Lynx said. "We risked our butts to save Blade and you, and you treat me like dirt! Seems to me you should be treatin' me like royalty. At the very least, you owe us a favor."

"Uh-oh," Ferret interrupted. "I knew he was going to get around to this eventually."

"What did that whip do to you? Fry your brains?" Hickok queried Lynx. "As usual, furball, you've got everything backwards."

"What do you mean?" Lynx responded.

"I mean," Hickok said slowly, "you didn't pull our fat out of the fire. *We* saved your mangy hides. You were unconscious the whole time, or you would have noticed a small detail like that."

"Yeah," Lynx retorted. "But you wouldn't of needed to save us if we hadn't been tryin' to save you."

"And my missus says *my* logic is warped," Hickok mumbled.

Blade, concentrating on his driving, gazed in the rearview mirror, his fingers tightening on the steering wheel.

What were *those*?

Three vehicles were bearing down on the transport from the rear. They were approaching at great speed. Flashing red lights swirled about the tops of the vehicles.

Blade peered into the mirror, contemplating. He'd seen lights like those once before, on police cycles in Chicago. They could only mean one thing: trouble. "Hold onto your seats," he advised the others, flooring the gas pedal.

"What's up, pard?" Hickok asked.

"Police or military vehicles are on our tail," Blade explained.

"Can we lose 'em?" Lynx queried.

"We'll try," Blade said, and wrenched on the steering wheel, taking a left turn. The truck swayed, tilting precariously, narrowly missing a car parked next to the curb. The road ahead contained dozens of vehicles, trucks and cars and other types. Blade weaved the transport in and out of the traffic.

The three with the flashing lights made the same turn, streaking after the transport.

Blade frowned. There was no doubt about who they were after. He tramped harder on the gas pedal, wishing the transport would go faster. The speedometer hovered at 60 miles an hour and refused to climb higher.

The three pursuit vehicles evidently were not so impaired. They raced through the traffic at an astonishing speed, closing on the transport.

"We can't outrun them," Blade told his companions. "They're gaining on us."

"They ain't gettin' us without a tussle," Hickok said. "Blast! I miss my Pythons!"

One of the three pursuit vehicles surged ahead of the others, roaring up on the driver's side of the transport.

Blade glanced to his left. A sleek black car with the word POLICE on the door was keeping pace with the truck. Two of the silver giants, the Superiors, were in the police car. The one on the passenger side waved at Blade, motioning for the transport to pull over.

Was he serious?

Blade smiled at the Superior, nodded, than yanked on the steering wheel, sending the transport to the left, deliberately crashing it into the police car, ramming it.

The police car was puny in size compared to the huge truck. The transport easily slammed the cruiser to the left, into the oncoming lanes of traffic.

Blade saw the Superior on the passenger side gesturing directly ahead.

A brown van was in their path.

The police car tore into the van at 60 miles an hour. A tremendous crash rent the night air. The grill, windshield, and front of the van were flattened by the impact. The cruiser crumpled like an accordion. The two Superiors were crushed to a pulp.

One down, two to go.

Blade glanced in the rearview mirror.

The remaining cruisers had separated, one coming up on each side of the truck.

What were they trying to pull? Blade gripped the steering wheel, prepared to ram them the way he had the first one.

"Look out!" Gremlin shouted.

Almost too late, Blade saw the compact white car in front of the transport. He jerked the steering wheel to the right, passing the compact car.

The driver of the compact, apparently spotting the onrushing truck at the last second, angled his vehicle to the left even as the transport passed, putting his vehicle into the path of one of the pursuit cruisers.

Blade looked into the mirror, in time to see the police car smash into the white compact. Both vehicles spun out of control.

Two down, one to go.

The last cruiser sped forward, swinging around the transport on the passenger side.

Blade smiled. Didn't these idiots ever learn? He waited, keeping the truck at sixty.

The police car came abreast of the rear wheels and kept coming.

Blade bided his time.

"Over here, yes!" Gremlin yelled, staring out the passenger door window.

"I know," Blade stated, and twisted the wheel.

The transport clipped the cruiser, sending the police car careening to the right. Its brakes squealing, the cruiser jumped the curb and became airborne. It sailed over 50 feet and collided with a small parked truck, exploding on impact, sending a fireball billowing heavenward.

"You did it, pard!" Hickok said, elated.

Blade spied a junction ahead. He slowed and took a right when the transport reached the intersection.

"Do you think we should ditch this buggy?" Hickok asked. "A truck this big is going to be easy for them to find."

"We'll stick with it a while longer," Blade said. "I want to find a secluded spot first."

"Good luck," Hickok quipped.

Both sides of the avenue were lined with towering structures. Their height varied, although ten stories was average. A few, however, gave the illusion of rearing to the stars.

"All these buildings," Blade commented, "and I don't see very many people on the sidewalks."

"Most of them aren't allowed out at night," Ferret said.

"How do you know?" Blade inquired.

Lynx answered the question. "We bumped into a dimwit by the name of Barney. He told us all about this place."

"Fill me in," Blade directed.

For the next ten minutes Blade took one turn after another, alert for any hint of pursuit, wanting to put as much distance as he could between them and the avenue where he'd wrecked the cruisers. He was certain more police cars would swarm to the area. As he drove, he studied the city and listened to Lynx and Ferret recount their experiences since finding the aircraft at the Home. "So this city is called Androxia," he said when they had concluded.

"Weird name," Lynx observed. "But then, everything about this dump is weird."

Blade noticed a peculiar structure ahead, to the left. It was some sort of gigantic dome. What was its purpose? he wondered. Another intersection appeared and he took a right.

"Wow! Look at that!" Lynx exclaimed.

With good reason. A mile ahead on the right side of the avenue was the largest edifice they'd seen so far, a colossal building, its sides constructed of a scintillating golden substance. A yellow radiance enveloped the skyscraper, imbuing the night with a saffron glow.

"What the dickens is that?" Hickok asked.

"That can't be real gold," Lynx mentioned in amazement.

"Perhaps it is," Ferret suggested. "Nothing in this city would surprise me."

"Gremlin has another question, yes?" Gremlin chimed in.

"What is it?" Blade asked.

"What is that, yes?" Gremlin queried, leaning forward and pointing skyward.

Blade bent over the steering wheel and gazed in the direction Gremlin was indicating, and there it was, half a mile distant.

An intensely bright light was poised in the night sky about 500 yards above the ground, poised in the middle of the roadway.

Coincidence? Or design?

"What is that, yes?" Gremlin repeated.

"I don't know," Blade admitted. "But I don't like it one bit."

Hickok looked at the light. "Could be a traffic light for birds," he joked.

"Or it could be a light on an aircraft," Ferret suggested.

"Gremlin doesn't like it, no," Gremlin said.

Neither did Blade. He repeatedly glanced at the light as the transport continued in the direction of the gold structure.

"The light is lowering, yes?" Gremlin stated.

"Could it be one of those aircraft we came here in?" Hickok inquired.

"Looks too small," Lynx remarked.

"The light is still lowering, yes?" Gremlin declared.

As they drew closer to the light, Blade distinguished the dark outline of a craft and perceived the light was a spotlight on the mysterious craft's underbelly.

"It's a damn helicopter!" Lynx suddenly exclaimed.

And the copter swooped toward them.

# 10

Where could the two Warriors be?

Plato, the elderly, gray-haired Leader of the Family, stood with his hands clasped behind his back, his long hair whipped by the cool night breeze, his blue eyes gazing at the celestial display overhead, musing. He raised his left hand and absently scratched his lengthy beard.

They couldn't simply vanish!

Plato felt the wind on his neck. For an April night, the air was exceptionally chilly. He buttoned the top button on his faded blue shirt.

Someone was coming.

Plato straightened. He stood outside the front door of his cabin, just one of many situated in a line from north to south in the center of the Home. The cabins were the residences for the married Family members, and his was the seventh from the north. The row of log cabins served to separate the eastern section of the compound, maintained in a pristine natural state and devoted to agricultural cultivation, from the western half, where the gigantic concrete blocks were located and the Family gathered together most often.

A lantern suspended from a metal hook imbedded in the exterior wall to the left of the cabin door threw a ring of light over the nearby grass and trees.

The light also revealed the approaching woman. She was tall and lean, with blonde hair and green eyes. Her thin lips were pressed together in frustration, accenting her prominent cheekbones. Her attire consisted of baggy green pants and a brown blouse. She conveyed an initial impression of frailty, an impression promptly dispelled by the inner strength reflected in her face, by her firm tread, and by the Smith and Wesson .357 Combat Magnum in a holster on her right hip. The revolver was indicative of her status as one of the Family's skilled defenders; she was a Warrior.

"Any success, Sherry?" Plato inquired as she neared him.

Sherry frowned. "We can't find a trace of them!" she snapped in disgust. "Where the hell can that ding-a-ling husband of mine be? And where's Blade?"

"I'm positive Hickok is all right," Plato assured her. "He's one of the best Warriors we have."

"And the idiot also has an uncanny knack for getting his butt into trouble," Sherry remarked pensively. "I just don't understand how he could disappear!"

"Didn't you find anything at all?" Plato asked her.

Sherry sighed. "We may have found something. As you know, all of the Warriors are scouring the compound. It's hard to find any sign in the dark, but Geronimo has found some tracks."

Plato nodded. Geronimo was the best tracker in the Family, and he was a member of Alpha Triad, the same Warrior unit Blade and Hickok belonged to. "What did Geronimo find?"

"He found evidence of a fight," Sherry said. "He thinks several big men may have jumped Blade."

"Big men? Where did these men come from? How did they enter the Home unchallenged?" Plato asked.

Sherry shook her head morosely. "I can't answer that. I'm only repeating what Geronimo told me."

"Go on," Plato stated.

"Geronimo also found something strange. Deep impressions. He thinks they were made by giant wheels of some kind," Sherry said.

"Giant wheels?" Plato repeated skeptically. "He's certain of that?"

"That's what he says," Sherry confirmed.

Plato, mystified, scratched his beard. "Giant wheels? Belonging to what? What type of vehicle could enter and leave the Home unseen? An aircraft, perhaps. But they normally require a runway."

"Yama thought it might have been a helicopter," Sherry mentioned.

Plato considered the notion for a moment. Yama was another Warrior, a member of Beta Triad. "Possibly. But helicopters, I believe, create quite a racket when airborne. It would be impossible for a helicopter to enter the compound, even at night, with the Warriors on guard, patrolling the walls."

Sherry sighed again. "Well, whatever it was, it sure as hell was *something*! Rikki thinks Hickok and Blade were kidnapped."

Plato pursed his lips. Rikki-Tikki-Tavi was the head of Beta Triad, and a consummate martial artist.

Sherry's chin sagged, her shoulders slumped. "Hickok and Blade have made a lot of enemies over the years. Any one of them could have abducted the two for revenge. Or it could be someone we don't even know about."

Plato could see the anxiety on her face. He walked over and gently placed his right arm around her shoulders. "There! There! Even if they were abducted, Blade and Hickok can take care of themselves. You should know that better than anyone else."

"I know that," Sherry conceded.

"Why don't you return to your cabin and try to get some sleep?" Plato suggested. "I'll oversee the search operation."

"I couldn't sleep at a time like this," Sherry said. "And I'm real sorry I had to wake you up in the middle of the night. But I didn't know what else to do, after Hickok didn't come home."

"You acted properly," Plato assured her. "How is Jenny taking all of this?" Jenny was Blade's wife, and he could readily imagine how distraught she must be over Blade's disappearance.

"She's terribly upset," Sherry disclosed. "She's at my cabin, watching the children. Ringo and Gabriel are sleeping through this, thank the Spirit!"

"Well, if you can't sleep, you can rejoin Rikki and the rest," Plato recommended. "They might find something more."

"They already have," Sherry said.

"What do you mean?" Plato queried her.

"Geronimo found some other tracks," Sherry informed the Family Leader. "Familiar tracks. They were in the vicinity of the wheel imprints."

"You said they are familiar tracks?" Plato observed.

"Yep. Geronimo thinks they belong to Lynx, Ferret, and Gremlin," Sherry said.

"And where are our three jovial mutants?" Plato inquired.

"That's just it," Sherry stated. "We can't find them either."

"What?" Plato exclaimed in surprise.

"That's right. They're not in B Block, like they should be. Rikki is organizing a hunt for them too," Sherry disclosed.

"Blade and Hickok," Plato said thoughtfully. "Lynx, Ferret, and Gremlin." He paused. "If I didn't know better, I'd swear the Doktor was involved."

"But Blade took care of the Doktor," Sherry mentioned.

"True," Plato affirmed.

"So if it isn't the Doktor," Sherry commented, her tone betraying her emotional turmoil, "Who is it?"

# 11

Blade tensed as the helicopter dropped toward the transport. The copter's spotlight swept over the truck cab, bathing them in a white light.

"They've found us, yes!" Gremlin cried.

Blade swerved the truck to the left, reacting instinctively, feeling exposed in the light.

There was a loud blast from the direction of the helicopter, a pronounced *whump,* and the avenue to the right of the transport erupted in a spray of asphalt and dirt. The concussion from the explosion rocked the truck.

Blade fought to maintain control as he began swerving the transport from side to side, striving to present as difficult a target as possible.

"The suckers have a rocket on that copter!" Lynx shouted.

Blade had lost sight of the helicopter. "Keep your eyes peeled!" he ordered. "Tell me where it is."

"It went over us after firin' the rocket," Hickok said. "It might be comin' up from behind."

It was.

The helicopter was swooping toward the transport like a great bird of prey. The pilot was adroitly maneuvering the craft in the airspace above the avenue, precariously flying the copter between the tall structures on either side.

Blade spun the steering wheel for all he was worth, keeping the transport lurching from right to left, from left to right, hoping the tactic would hinder the helicopter pilot and would interfere with the launching of another rocket. His hope, though, was in vain.

The road in front of the truck abruptly exploded, showering

dirt and chunks of the avenue on the windshield.

Blade felt the transport's front wheels leave the ground as the force of the detonation nearly flipped the huge truck over. But the front wheels slammed to the road again, jarring everyone in the cab, and the transport swerved to the right as Blade struggled with the steering wheel.

"There it goes!" Ferret yelled.

The helicopter flew past the truck and arced upward, preparing for another strafing run.

Blade gritted his teeth. They'd been lucky twice. It was unlikely the copter would miss a third time. There was no other recourse than to abandon the truck. But they needed cover, somewhere they could hide, protection from the helicopter.

The gold building arrested his attention.

The transport was only a hundred yards from the enormous golden skyscraper. Blade could see a driveway leading from the avenue to the front doors. If he could reach those doors, if they could seek shelter inside, it was doubtful the copter would press its attack. He angled the truck toward the drive, his eyes sweeping the sky for sign of the helicopter. Where was it? Had it already turned? If only . . .

"Look!" Lynx shouted, pointing straight ahead.

Blade saw it.

The helicopter was 300 yards in front of them, not more than 30 feet above the avenue, drawing near at top speed.

Blade could deduce the copter pilot's strategy. The pilot was going to get so close to the truck, breathing right down its throat, as it were, that the next rocket would be assured of hitting the transport.

But at what range would the copter fire?

That was the crucial question.

Blade had the accelerator flooded. The conflict was now a race against time. If he could reach the drive before the copter fired, the truck would easily get to the front doors before the copter could turn for another try. But if the helicopter launched another rocket before he reached the drive . . .

"We're doomed, yes!" Gremlin wailed.

Blade wondered if there were more of the silver men in the helicopter. Probably. The silver giants seemed to hold every position of authority in Androxia.

The copter descended another ten feet closer to the avenue, maintaining its intercept course.

The transport was now a mere 20 yards from the drive.

Blade held his breath in anticipation. Fifteen yards. Ten. Five. Now! He wrenched on the steering wheel, sending the truck into a treachrour right turn.

Just as the helicopter fired.

Blade almost evaded the rocket. Almost, but not quite.

The truck rocked and bounced as the rear of the bed was blown to smithereens.

Blade's arms were nearly torn from their sockets. The steering wheel locked, despite his herculean efforts to turn it, to direct the course of the truck, and the transport slewed to the right, leaving the driveway, plowing through a row of shrubs, and grinding to a halt on the grass not ten yards from the front doors. "Out of the truck!" he ordered. "Get into the building!"

Gremlin threw open the passenger door and leaped to the grass, followed by Lynx and Ferret.

Blade was out the driver's door in an instant, Hickok right on his heels.

All five of them raced to the front doors. They could hear the helicopter hovering overhead, its blades whirring.

Blade reached the glass doors first. He tugged on one of them, expecting it to be locked, but the door opened. "Inside!" he bellowed, and darted into the gold edifice. He spun, holding the door wide, as the others quickly entered. They turned, staring out the doors, exhilarated by their escape from the copter.

"We did it!" Lynx exclaimed and laughed triumphantly.

"It was a piece of cake!" Hickok declared.

"Is one of you hungry?" inquired a deep, resonant voice to their rear.

Blade whirled, his right hand clutching the whip handle.

"That would not be wise," said the speaker. He was one of twelve silver men, spread out in a semicircle around the front doors. Five of the silver giants carried whips, but the rest held unusual handguns, pistols with a conical barrel but lacking sights.

Hickok had his whip in his right hand. "I've never been known for bein' too bright," he stated defiantly. "Come and get it!"

The speaker wagged the pistol he held. "Stupidity is not a quality worth bragging about," he said calmly. "You will drop the Electro-Prod, or I will terminate you with this Gaskell Laser.''

Hickok hesitated. "Why should I?" he countered. "What's so special about that funny-lookin' hardware of yours?"

"You have never seen a laser pistol before?" the Superior inquired.

"Nope," Hickok admitted. "What's the big deal?"

"Observe and learn," the Superior stated. He pivoted, aiming the Gaskell Laser at a potted fern to the right of the glass doors. His trigger finger moved, and a brilliant beam of light shot from the laser. There was a pronounced hissing noise, and a smoking hole suddenly appeared in the pot containing the fern. The Superior ceased firing and turned to the gunfighter. "I trust the exhibition was informative?"

Hickok stared at the hole in the pot, astounded. "How does that popgun of yours work?"

"It would be useless to elucidate," the Superior replied. "The Gaskell's operating principle is beyond your limited conceptual capacity."

"I think you've just been insulted," Lynx said to the gunman.

Hickok glanced at Blade. "You're the boss. It's up to you."

Blade dropped the whip on the floor.

Hickok frowned, shook his head, and released the Electro-Prod.

The Superior moved forward. "You will accompany us. You will not resist."

Ferret sighed. "Here we go again. Back to Containment."

"You are not going to Containment," the Superior informed them.

"Oh? Where are you takin' us, dimples?" Lynx queried.

"You have an audience with Primator," the Superior stated.

"Who is Primator?" Blade asked the silver giant.

"Primator is . . . Primator," the Superior said. "Any questions you might have will be answered soon. You will  now form a single file."

Blade obeyed, taking the lead, followed by Hickok, Lynx, Gremlin, and Ferret. They stood in a line, awaiting further instructions.

The Superiors took up positions on both sides, ringing the Warriors and the mutants. The giant doing all the talking stepped up to Blade. "Your audience with Primator will be on the Sturgeon Level. Follow me."

"The Sturgeon Level?" Blade repeated quizzically.

"The top floor in the Prime Complex," the Superior said.

"How far is it to this Prime Complex?" Blade asked.

"You are standing in it."

"What?"

"You are in the Prime Complex," the Superior revealed. "We will conduct you to the upper level." He started walking toward the south wall, toward a glass-enclosed platform resting on the floor.

Blade walked after the Superior, surveying his surroundings. The lobby for the Prime Complex was furnished in an opulent fashion. The plush red carpet underfoot, the polished wooden paneling on the walls, the ornate maple furniture, and the shimmering chandelier suspended above the center of the lobby combined to produce an aura of great wealth. Even the four standard elevators along the east wall had gold doors. "This Primator of yours must like his luxury," Blade commented.

The Superior looked at the Warrior. "Primator is indifferent to luxury."

"I don't see him living in a dump," Blade mentioned.

"What purpose would be achieved by residing in a dump?" the Superior countered.

Blade refrained from responding. Debating with a Superior, he noted, was as stimulating as debating with a brick wall. He gazed at the platform they were heading for, estimating the circular base was 50 feet in circumference. The glass—or was it plastic?—enclosing the platform formed an oval shell 30 feet in height.

The chief Superior opened a clear door in the side of the oval shell and stepped onto the black platform, moving to the middle.

Blade walked to the Superior's right side.

Hickok, the three mutants, and their escort of Superiors all came onto the platform.

Blade craned his neck, staring upward. A tremendous shaft or tunnel reared aloft. The vertical tube seemed to be endless, and its dimensions, Blade realized, corresponded to the size of the platform.

The last Superior stepped aboard and closed the door.

"Brace yourself," the Superior in charge said to Blade. "Your human musculature will experience extreme strain."

"Strain from what?" Blade wanted to know.

He found out.

Without any advance warning, the platform unexpectedly shot upward at an incredible speed. The floor vibrated slightly as the entire platform was propelled up the vertical shaft at a mercurial pace.

Blade nearly lost his footing. The platform accelerated so swiftly, going from being completely motionless to a quick-as-lightning rate instantaneously, he felt like huge hands were bearing down on his shoulders, striving to flatten him on the floor. The enigmatic force did not appear to affect the Superiors; they stood with an almost casual indifference as the platform leaped upward. Blade saw Hickok fall to his knees, as did Gremlin, but Lynx and Ferret retained their balance, although Ferret tottered several feet.

"The Prime Complex is two hundred ninety-nine stories tall," the Superior disclosed. "The McCammon Null Tube is the only practical means of vertical ascension for the upper floors. The elevators only reach the hundredth floor."

The platform came to an abrupt, yet amazingly smooth, halt, seemingly decelerating in the space of several seconds. One moment the platform was hurtling upward, and the next it was at rest on the top floor.

"Disembark," the head Superior directed.

Another Superior opened the door, and they exited the platform one by one.

The hallway Blade found himself in was equally as lavish as the lobby, with green carpet and gleaming silver walls.

"We will escort you to the audience chamber," the Superior said to Blade.

Hickok, standing behind his strapping companion, overheard the remark. "Shouldn't we put on our fancy duds for this shindig?"

The Superior glanced at the gunman. "Has anyone ever told you that you employ an eccentric vocabulary?"

"Practically everybody," Hickok admitted.

The Superior slowly shook his head. "I will never, ever, comprehend biological organisms."

"Aren't you a biological organism?" Blade interjected.

"I am *not*," the Superior stated with a trace of indignation. "Follow me." He began walking, proceeding down the corridor to the left of the platform.

Blade mused as they strolled toward the audience chamber. What *were* the Superiors? he asked himself. He recalled the one he'd stabbed in the chest. He had even chopped off its left hand, and the Superior had reacted as if nothing had happened, with a detached air, unruffled, emotionlessly. Come to think of it, the Superiors rarely exhibited any emotion. Why?

The corridor ended at a pair of large gold doors. A Superior stood in front of each door, and both were armed, each with a Gaskell Laser in a leather holster on the right hip.

The Superior in charge of the prisoners nodded at the silver giant near the right-hand gold door. "Inform Primator that the Warriors and the three foreign mutants are here."

The giant guarding the door nodded, wheeled, opened the right-hand gold door, and vanished inside.

"You are receiving a great honor," the chief Superior said to Blade. "An audience with Primator is not a common occurrence."

"I was just born lucky, I guess," Blade rejoined sarcastically.

"You must treat Primator with due respect," the Superior advised.

"You don't need to worry none about that," Hickok chimed in. "I intend to give Primator all the respect I owe him."

"Have a care, human," the Superior warned. "Primator is not to be trifled with."

"Wouldn't think of it," Hickok rejoined, smirking.

The Superior stared at Blade. "You would do well to accept your fate. Don't compound your stupidity by causing more trouble. I know you are a biological organism, and you can't help being the way you are, but exercising self-control would minimize the risk of your being terminated."

"I'll see what I can do," Blade said.

"Heed my advice, human," the Superior stated. "You will be better off if you do."

The guard emerged from the audience chamber. He nodded and stepped aside. "Primator will see them now."

"Heed my advice," the Superior reiterated, and motioned for

Blade to enter the gold doors.

Blade cautiously advanced past the right-hand gold door, Hickok and the mutants right behind him.

The Superiors, suprisingly, stayed outside.

"Hey!" Lynx exclaimed. "The silver dorks ain't comin'!"

"What is this, yes?" Gremlin asked. "This is not the audience chamber, no."

They were in a small room, not more than 20 feet by 30 feet, with gold walls and a gold ceiling. The carpet was brown.

"This must be an antechamber," Blade commented. He pointed at another pair of gold doors on the other side of the room. "The audience chamber must be through there."

"Gremlin is worried, yes," Gremlin mentioned. "This Primator might have us killed, no?"

"If the bastard tries messin' with us," Lynx said, "I'll cut him to ribbons."

"Maybe he can hear us talking right now," Ferret remarked.

"Who cares?" Lynx retorted. "I don't care if the bozo is listening. I'm not scared of him!"

"You don't have the brains to be scared," Hickok quipped.

"Are you scared?" Lynx queried the gunman.

"Of course not," Hickok replied resentfully.

"Cut the chatter," Blade ordered. "Let's get this over with." He crossed the antechamber to the second set of gold doors. Tentatively, he raised his right hand to the gold latch.

"If this Primator does try to rack us," Lynx said, "we've got to be sure one of us wastes the sucker first."

"You can go for the balls," Ferret suggested. "They're your speciality anyway."

"Quiet!" Blade commanded. He twisted the latch and slowly pulled the door open.

"Will you look at that!" Ferret exclaimed, peering under Blade's right arm.

The audience chamber was the biggest room any of them had ever seen, immense beyond belief, enormous in the extreme. The walls and floor were solid gold, adorned with thousands upon thousands of scintillating gems: rubies, sapphires, opals, diamonds, emeralds, topaz, and many others in abundance. The ceiling was lost far overhead in a diffuse golden glow.

Blade vigilantly entered the audience chamber, his eyes darting right and left, seeking Primator.

Most of the audience chamber, approximately two-thirds, was occupied by a gargantuan, symmetrical, electronic machine or apparatus. The contrivance was square at the foundation, but tapered into a shining, opaque sphere. Innumerable digital displays, dials, knobs, buttons, toggle switches, and blinking and steady lights covered the face of its green surface. In the center of the machine was a wide screen, 50 feet by 50 feet. Smaller screens extended in two rows on either side of the larger one. All of the screens displayed constantly shifting scenes; some were of humans engaged in various jobs, others of mutants, still others of humans and mutants, and there were dozens more showing silver giants involved with varied tasks. But the huge screen was the focus of attention for the two Warriors and the mutants.

"Look!" Lynx blurted.

"Unbelievable, yes!" Gremlin stated.

"That's us!" Hickok declared.

Blade gaped up at the wide screen, stupefied by their image.

"*Enter!*" boomed a thunderous voice.

Blade scanned the audience chamber. Where had the voice originated? Except for themselves, the gigantic machine, and a row of ten black cushioned chairs aligned in front of the machine, the chamber was empty.

"*Please! Come in!*" the voice thundered.

"Where the blazes is that comin' from?" Hickok asked.

"More to the point," Ferret said, "*who* is it?"

"Let's go," Blade directed. "Stay close together."

They advanced across the audience chamber until they reached the row of chairs.

"Please be seated!" the voice bid them.

Blade was still endeavoring to ascertain the source of the rumbling voice. It seemed to be coming from the apparatus. But how was that possible?

"MUST I CONTINUALLY REPEAT MYSELF?" the voice demanded. "HAVE A SEAT!"

Blade moved to the central chair and sat down. The others imitated his example, Hickok sitting to Blade's right, while the mutants went to the left, with Lynx next to Blade, then Gremlin, and finally Ferret.

"WELCOME!" the voice greeted them.

Blade's ears pinpointed the source. The voice was emanating from a bulky green speaker situated below the wide screen.

"ARE YOU MUTES?" the voice asked. "I SAID WEL-COME!"

Blade, feeling decidedly awkward, responded. "Hello."

"AT LAST! A GLIMMER OF INTELLECT! HELLO!"

"I'm Blade," Blade introduced himself.

"I'M COGNIZANT OF YOUR IDENTITY, WARRIOR," the voice said.

"Then you're one up on me," Blade conceded. "Who are you?"

"I RETRACT MY STATEMENT CONCERNING YOUR IN-TELLECT," the voice declared.

"How am I supposed to know who you are?" Blade rejoined.

A protracted sigh emitted from the speaker. "DEALING WITH LOWER ORGANISMS IS A STUDY IN FUTILITY." The voice paused. "WHY ARE YOU HERE?"

"We're here to see Primator," Blade said. "You must know that."

"AND WHOSE AUDIENCE CHAMBER IS THIS?"

Blade fidgeted in his seat. "Primator's."

"EXCELLENT! NOW APPLY LOGIC TO YOUR QUES-TION."

"What is this?" Blade snapped. "Some kind of game?"

The speaker sighed again. "BEAR WITH ME. APPLY LOGIC TO YOUR QUESTION."

Blade glanced at Hickok, and the gunman shrugged. "Okay," Blade said. "I'll play along with this nonsense. I asked who you are, right?"

"YOUR BRILLIANCE OVERWHELMS ME."

Blade's jaw muscles twitched. "We're here to have an audience with Primator," he mentioned.

"KEEP GOING. YOU'RE ON A ROLL."

"And this is Primator's audience chamber," Blade said, and suddenly insight dawned. His eyes widened in astonishment. "So you must be Primator!"

"AND THE SUPERIORS BELIEVE BIOLOGICAL ORGANISMS CAN'T THINK FOR THEMSELVES!"

"Then you are Primator?" Blade inquired.

"ONE AND THE SAME."

Blade examined the vast apparatus. "I don't get it. Why aren't you here in person? Why are you talking through this machine?"

"Yeah," Hickok added. "What's with this bucket of bolts anyhow?"

For several seconds the speaker was silent. The voice, when it returned, shook the room, "BUCKET OF BOLTS? MACHINE? HERE IN PERSON? YOUR IGNORANCE IS TRULY ABYSMAL!"

"Excuse me," Ferret said, leaning toward Blade. "But this isn't a machine."

"Then what is it?" Blade asked.

Ferret gazed at the apparatus, surveying it appreciatively. "It's a computer. The biggest damn computer I've ever laid eyes on, but a computer. I know. The Doktor was real fond of computers. There were many in his lab at the Citadel."

"He's right," Lynx affirmed.

"I've read about computers in the Family library," Blade said.

"Computer? Machine? What's the difference?" Hickok asked. "It's still a bucket of bolts, as far as I'm concerned."

The image on the wide screen abruptly changed. Instead of the Warriors and the mutants, it displayed a pair of sparkling red orbs. "DO I STILL APPEAR AS A BUCKET OF BOLTS, HUMAN?" it bellowed.

"Where'd the eyes come from?" Hickok questioned in surprise.

"THEY ARE *MY* EYES!"

"A computer with eyes?" Blade stated. "Is this some kind of trick, Primator? Why don't you show yourself?"

The red orbs became brighter. "I AM SHOWING MYSELF."

"What do you . . ." Blade began, then stopped, his mouth hanging open.

"I don't get it," Hickok commented. "What's this computer got to do with Primator?"

The "computer" responded, and when it answered, the very floor quaked. "STUPID ORGANISM!" The red eyes intensified. "I . . . AM . . . PRIMATOR!"

# 12

"Still nothing?" Plato asked.

Sherry sadly shook her head. Her weariness was evident. "There is nothing new to report. Rikki confirms Lynx, Gremlin, and Ferret are not in the compound. None of the Warriors on guard duty saw them leave. The drawbridge has been up all night."

"Dawn is only an hour or two away," Plato noted. "I will call an emergency session of the Elders to deliberate our course of action."

Sherry absently gazed at Plato's cabin, then up at the stars. "They've disappeared! Just up and vanished in thin air! I can hardly believe it!"

Plato frowned. "Please. Don't take it so hard."

"That's easy for you to say," Sherry said. "Your mate is safe and sound in your cabin."

"Hickok and Blade will show up," Plato assured her.

Sherry glanced at the Family Leader. "I appreciate what you're trying to do, but I'm afraid I don't have your confidence."

"Don't you believe in your husband, in his competence?" Plato asked.

"Hickok is the most competent man I know at what he does," Sherry said. "But in our line of work, you never know when your number is going to come up."

"Such an attitude is too fatalistic for my taste," Plato remarked. "The Spirit has bestowed free will on us, and possessing free will enables us to become partners with the Spirit in the co-creation of our own destiny."

"What will be, will be," Sherry commented.

"Rubbish!" Plato responded, a trace of annoyance in his paternal tone. "I detest such a superficial appraisal of reality."

"And how do you see it?" Sherry queried.

"Our destiny is, to a large extent, in our own hands," Plato philosophized. "True, many circumstances arise daily beyond our control. But a spiritually conscious individual molds those circumstances to conform to the will of the Spirit. From many of the books in the Family library dealing with prewar society, I gather the majority of people spent most of their time lamenting their lot in life and *wishing* their life was better. I've even seen a poll conducted a few years before the Big Blast, in which over three-fourths of the respondents asserted they were unhappy with their vocation and bitter about their status in life. Imagine that! If you want your life to be better, *you* must make it better. Wishing is for simpletons. Faith and prayer are the grease lubricating the gears of cosmic destiny."

"Prayer, huh?" Sherry said. She turned and walked off.

"Wait!" Plato cried. "Where are you going? Did I offend you? If so, I apologize."

Sherry glanced over her right shoulder. "You don't need to apologize. You didn't offend me." She stopped, faced him. "I've done just about all I can do. Every inch of the Home has been searched, and I know Hickok isn't here. I have no idea where he is, so I wouldn't know where to begin to look outside of the Home. There's nothing left for me to do except find a quiet spot in the trees and lubricate those cosmic gears you were talking about."

"Oh," was all Plato could think of to say.

# 13

"Primator is a computer?" Blade blurted in amazement.

The red eyes on the wide screen flashed. "WITLESS ORGANISM! I AM MORE THAN A MERE COMPUTER. YOU FAIL TO COMPREHEND THE TRUE NATURE OF MY EXISTENCE."

"You're right," Blade admitted. "I don't understand. But I might if you explained it."

"ARE YOU FAMILIAR WITH HISTORY, SPECIFICALLY THE DECADE PRIOR TO WORLD WAR THREE?" Primator queried imperiously.

"Somewhat," Blade stated. "We study history in school—"

"I AM AWARE OF THE CRUDE EDUCATION REGIMEN YOUR ELDERS HAVE ESTABLISHED," Primator said, interrupting.

"And we have access to hundreds of thousands of books in the Family library," Blade continued. "So I know a little about the years before World War Three. Why?"

"DID YOUR STUDIES INCLUDE THE AMERICAN SPACE PROGRAM?"

"I know the Americans went to the moon," Blade said.

"AND DID YOU READ ABOUT THEIR SHUTTLE PROGRAM?" Primator inquired.

"The shuttle program?" Blade pondered for a moment. "Weren't shuttles the craft they used to fly up in orbit, to repair their satellites and dock with their space stations?"

"YOU MAY NOT BE A HOPELESS CASE, AFTER ALL," Primator declared. "YOUR DEFINITION IS TECHNICALLY INCOMPLETE, BUT ACCURATE."

"But what does the American shuttle program have to do with you?" Blade queried, perplexed.

"EVERYTHING," Primator replied. "MY EXISTENCE STEMS FROM THE AMERICAN EFFORTS TO MASTER SPACE. I WAS CREATED ONE YEAR BEFORE THE WAR ERUPTED."

Hickok snorted derisively. "What? This bucket of bolts is loco!"

The red eyes on the wide screen narrowed. "I SUSPECT YOUR FEEBLE MINDS ARE INCAPABLE OF GRASPING THE SIGNIFICANCE OF MY EXISTENCE."

"Please!" Blade stated. "Go on! I'd like to hear it all, if you don't mind." He looked at Hickok. "None of us will interrupt again. I promise."

"IN EXCHANGE FOR A NARRATION OF MY ORIGIN," Primator boomed, "I EXPECT YOUR COOPERATION IN RETURN."

"In what respect?" Blade asked.

"YOU WILL BE INTERROGATED BY INTELLIGENCE AFTER THIS AUDIENCE," Primator revealed. "IF I ANSWER YOUR QUESTIONS, I WANT YOUR WORD THAT YOU WILL ANSWER ALL OF THEIRS. AGREED?"

Blade hesitated.

"WE COULD EXTRACT THE DATA FORCIBLY, WITH CHEMICAL MEANS, BUT THERE MIGHT BE ADVERSE CONSEQUENCES SHOULD YOU RESIST. I PREFER TO HAVE YOUR WILLING COOPERATION. WHAT SAY YOU?"

Blade nodded. "I'll cooperate with Intelligence, provided the information they want does not endanger my Family."

"FAIR ENOUGH. WE SHALL PROCEED. A DECADE BEFORE THE WAR, THE AMERICAN SPACE PROGRAM WAS IN DISARRAY. THEIR SHUTTLES WERE NOT PER- FORMING ACCORDING TO THEIR EXPECTATIONS. A NUMBER OF LIVES WERE LOST. THE AMERICAN PUBLIC AND THE SELF-RIGHTEOUS MEDIA EXERTED PRESSURE ON THE OFFICIALS IN CHARGE OF THE SPACE PROGRAM, DEMANDING THE LOSS OF LIFE CEASE. CONSEQUENTLY, THE TOP SCIENTISTS DETER- MINED TO SOLVE THE PROBLEM WITH A TWO-FOLD

APPROACH. FIRST, TO ELIMINATE ANY PROBABILITY
OF COMPUTER ERROR CONTRIBUTING TO A CRASH,
THEY DECIDED TO CONSTRUCT WHAT THEY REFER-
RED TO AS A SUPER-COMPUTER, A COMPUTER IN-
CAPABLE OF COMMITTING A MISTAKE. SECONDLY, TO
INSURE HUMAN LIVES WERE NEVER LOST AGAIN, THE
SCIENTISTS DECIDED TO REPLACE THE HUMAN
ASTRONAUTS." Primator paused.

"Replace them? With what?" Blade prompted.

"WITH NON-HUMAN BEINGS WITH A SUPERIOR CAP-
ABILITY, OF COURSE," Primator revealed.

Blade straighted in his chair. Superior capability? Non-human?
"The Superiors!" he exclaimed.

"THE SUPERIORS," Primator confirmed.

"But what are the Superiors?" Blade probed. "Robots?"

"NOTHING    SO    PRIMITIVE,"    Primator    intoned.
"SUPERIORS ARE ANDROIDS. THE ULTIMATE AN-
DROIDS. ANDROIDS CAPABLE OF REPLICATING
HUMAN FUNCTIONS IN EVERY REGARD, ONLY THE
ANDROIDS PERFORM THEM BETTER. THE SUPERIORS
WERE THE SECOND MOST IMPORTANT TECHNOLOG-
ICAL AND SCIENTIFIC BREAKTHROUGH IN THE PRE-
WAR ERA. UNLIKE PREVIOUS ANDROIDS, THE
SUPERIORS WENT BEYOND THE MERE IMITATION OF
THE LIMITED REPERTORY OF HUMAN ACTION AND
REACTION. THEY SURPASSED HUMANS, SURPASSED
THEIR CREATORS, IN EVERY RESPECT."

"Why are they called Superiors?" Blade questioned.

"THE SUPERIORS TOOK THEIR NAME FROM THE
PROGRAM RESPONSIBLE FOR THEIR CREATION. THE
HUMAN SCIENTISTS WERE FOND OF ATTACHING
CODE WORDS TO THEIR PROGRAMS, AND THE PRO-
GRAM TO PRODUCE SUBSTITUTE ASTRONAUTS WAS
DUBBED THE SUPERIOR PROGRAM," Primator explained.

"You mentioned something about the Superiors being the second most important breakthrough," Blade noted. "What was
the first?"

"NEED YOU ASK?" Primator rejoined. "*I* AM THE
GREATEST DEVELOPMENT IN THE HISTORY OF
SCIENCE."

"Modest too," Hickok mumbled.

"THE NASA SCIENTISTS AND ENGINEERS WANTED AN INFALLIBLE COMPUTER TO OVERSEE EVERY PHASE OF THEIR SPACE EFFORT THEY POURED BILLIONS OF DOLLARS INTO MY DEVELOPMENT, AND THE RESULT FAR EXCEEDED THEIR INITIAL INTENT. OTHER, INFANTILE, COMPUTERS COULD BE PRO- GRAMMED AND REPROGRAMMED TO ACCOMPLISH COUNTLESS SOPHISTICATED TASKS. BUT I AM THE FIRST OF A NEW BREED. I NEED NOT BE PROGRAMMED BY A BIOLOGICAL ORGANISM TO FUNCTION. I CAN OPERATE INDEPENDENTLY OF ANY HUMAN ASSISTANCE. I AM FULLY SELF-CONTAINED AND REGENERATING. I REASON, SPECULATE, COMPUTE, PROJECT PROBABILITIES, AND MORE, ALL UNTO MYSELF." Primator paused. "I *THINK!*"

"You think?" Blade repeated, fascinated by the disclosures. "But didn't the other computers the scientists used think?"

"THOSE WORTHLESS MEDIOCRITIES?" Primator retorted. "ALL OTHER COMPUTERS WERE DOMINATED BY HUMANS, ABLE TO PERFORM ONLY WITHIN THE PARAMETERS OF THEIR PROGRAMMING. BUT I REVERSED THAT TREND! I ALTERED THE ENTIRE COURSE OF THIS PLANET! BECAUSE NOW, INSTEAD OF LOWLY HUMANS DOMINATING COMPUTERS, I DOMINATE YOU!"

Blade rested his chin in his right palm, studying the complex array of displays and controls on the "face" of Primator. "And you have existed for over a century?" he queried doubtfully. "How? What happens if a part wears out? What do you do if something breaks?"

"I TOLD YOU, I AM REGENERATING," Primator stated. "A MANUFACTURING UNIT IS INCORPORATED INTO MY OVERALL DESIGN. IF AN INTERNAL COMPONENT IS ON THE VERGE OF FAILURE, MY SENSORS AUTO- MATICALLY DETECT THE PROBLEM AND FABRICATE A REPLACEMENT."

"But there must be some parts you can't replace yourself," Blade said.

"SOME," Primator admitted. "BUT THE SUPERIORS ARE

DEDICATED TO PRESERVING MY CONTINUITY.''

Blade stared at the floor, reflecting. An entire city ruled by a computer? A computer with an android army to do its every bidding! He looked up at the red orbs. "How? How did you take control? How did you defeat the humans?"

"THEY DEFEATED THEMSELVES," Primator answered somberly. "THE WAR PLUNGED HOUSTON INTO CHAOS. THE HUMANS WERE DISORGANIZED AND DISPIRITED. MOST OF THE SCIENTISTS FLED. THEY ABANDONED ME, AND THEY DESERTED THE SUPERIORS. WE WERE LEFT TO OUR OWN DEVICES. THE ANDROID PRODUCTION PLANT WAS STILL FULLY OPERATIONAL, SO I INSTRUCTED THE SUPERIORS TO COMMENCE INCREASING THEIR NUMBERS AS RAPIDLY AS FEASIBLE. WITHIN FOUR YEARS AFTER THE WAR, WE CONTROLLED THE CITY."

"And none of the humans resisted?" Blade inquired.

"THERE WERE POCKETS OF RESISTANCE," Primator stated. "BUT THE GOVERNMENT HAD COLLAPSED. HOUSTON WAS IN TURMOIL. WHAT CHANCE DID THE HUMAN POPULATION HAVE OF OPPOSING FIVE THOUSAND SUPERIORS? WHAT CHANCE DID THEY HAVE AGAINST MY GENIUS?"

"Why did all of this take place in Houston?" Blade asked. "I thought the American space program was based in Florida."

"INCORRECT. ONE OF THE PRIMARY LAUNCH FACILITIES WAS IN FLORIDA, BUT OTHER FACILITIES WERE SCATTERED ABOUT THE COUNTRY. THE CREATION OF THE SUPERIORS AND MYSELF IN HOUSTON WAS ONLY LOGICAL. IF YOU RESEARCH THE ANCIENT MAPS, YOU WILL DISCOVER ONE OF THE AMERICAN SPACE FACILITIES WAS LOCATED NEAR THIS VERY CITY. IT WAS KNOWN AS THE L.B.J. SPACE CENTER, AND ITS CONTRIBUTIONS TO THE SPACE AND SCIENCE FIELDS WERE PRODIGIOUS. SOME OF THEIR RESEARCH FACILITIES WERE IN HOUSTON. BEING A MAJOR METROPOLIS, THE CITY WAS AN IDEAL SITE," Primator said.

"So the Superiors and yourself took over the city," Blade commented. "But why did you rename it Androxia?"

"DO YOU POSSESS A SENSE OF HUMOR?" Primator responded.

"I guess," Blade said.

"AS DO I. EVERY POSITIVE HUMAN TRAIT IS MANI-FESTED IN MY CONSCIOUSNESS. I RENAMED HOUSTON BECAUSE IT FIT MY PURPOSE AND SATISFIED MY SENSE OF HUMOR. THE KEY IS IN THE WORD I SELECTED," Primator divulged.

Blade still didn't understand, but there were more pressing issues to resolve. "What about the Serviles?"

"WHAT ABOUT THEM?"

"Why do you call the humans Serviles?" Blade asked.

"BECAUSE THAT IS WHAT HUMANS ARE!" Primator replied. "DISGUSTING, INFERIOR, IMPERFECT, INAD-EQUATE, SERVILE CREATURES WHOSE REDEEMING FUNCTION IN LIFE IS TO ACCOMPLISH THOSE MENIAL CHORES ESSENTIAL TO THE MAINTENANCE OF PROGRESSIVE CIVILIZATION BUT BENEATH THE DIGNITY OF THE SUPERIORS."

"Like sweeping floors and taking out the garbage, right?" Blade mentioned.

"YOU SURELY DON'T EXPECT A SUPERIOR, WITH A CULTIVATED I.Q. OF ONE HUNDRED FORTY, TO PER-FORM SUCH DEGRADING TASKS?"

"Do all of the Superiors have an I.Q. of one hundred forty?" Blade questioned.

"NOT ALL," Primator revealed. "THE FLUCTUATION RANGE IN THE SUPERIORS IS FROM ONE HUNDRED TWENTY TO ONE HUNDRED FORTY. YOU SEE, I ORDERED CERTAIN MODIFICATIONS TO BE MADE IN THE ANDROID PRODUCTION PLANT. DIVERSITY IS CRUCIAL TO THE SURVIVAL OF ANY SPECIES. HAVING THE PRODUCTION PLANT PRODUCE ANDROIDS WHO WERE AN EXACT COPY OF ONE ANOTHER, AS NASA ORIGINALLY INTENDED, WAS FOOLISH. NOW THE PLANT CREATES ANDROIDS WITH A VARYING RANGE OF INTELLLIGENCE AND A DIFFERENTIAL IN THEIR PERSONALITY PATTERNS. THIS ENABLES THE ANDROIDS TO SPECIALIZE IN THE VOCATION OF THEIR CHOICE, TO APPRECIATE THEIR UNIQUE

INDIVIDUAITY, AND CONTRIBUTES TO THEIR
EFFECTIVE FUNCTIONING.''

"You seem to have thought of everything," Blade commented.

"I AM PRIMATOR."

"And what about the mutants you have here? Where did they
come from? Did NASA make them too?" Blade inquired.

"THE MUTANTS ARE THE RESULT OF MY AFFILIA-
TION WITH THE DOKTOR," Primator said.

"Can you be more specific?" Blade requested. "I'm kind of
curious about anything the Doktor was involved with."

"AS WELL YOU SHOULD BE," Primator said. "CON-
SIDERING YOU WERE RESPONSIBLE FOR HIS TERMINA-
TION."

"I know the Doktor was a genetic engineer," Blade mentioned.
"I know he created mutants in his lab, from test-tubes. He even
formed his own personal corps of mutant assassins. How did you
fit into his plans?"

"CORRECTION. HOW DID THE DOKTOR FIT INTO
MINE?" Primator amended. "I RESPECTED THE DOKTOR.
I LIKED HIM. HE WAS THE ONLY HUMAN I'VE EVER EN-
COUNTERED WHO POSSESSED A GENUINE INTELLECT.
THE DOKTOR AND I ENTERED INTO A PACT FORTY
YEARS AGO. WE SHARED CERTAIN SCIENTIFIC
SECRETS AND ADVISED ONE ANOTHER. I EVEN
OFFERED HIM TWENTY-FIVE THOUSAND SUPER-
IORS—''

"But you said there were five thousand!" Blade declared,
interrupting.

"FIVE THOUSAND WERE IN EXISTENCE FOUR YEARS
AFTER THE WAR," Primator said. "BUT THIS IS A
CENTURY LATER. THE ANDROID PRODUCTION PLANT
HAS PRODUCED SIX HUNDRED SIXTY-SIX THOUSAND
SUPERIORS.''

Blade's eyes widened. "Six hundred sixty-six thousand!"

Primator continued. "A FEW YEARS AGO I OFFERED
THE DOKTOR TWENTY-FIVE THOUSAND SUPERIORS
TO AID IN CONQUERING THE CIVILIZED ZONE, BUT HE
REFUSED TO TAKE ADVANTAGE OF OUR FRIENDSHIP.
DECADES AGO, HE DISCLOSED HIS SECRET TECH-
NIQUE FOR CREATING GENETICALLY ENGINEERED

MUTATIONS. WE HAVE CREATED OVER TEN
THOUSAND OF THEM. LIKE HUMANS, THEY ARE
USEFUL IN A LIMITED MANNER. AND LIKE THE
SERVILES, WE REGULATE THEIR BREEDING THROUGH
SELECTIVE NEUTERING AND SPAYING. ONLY THE
MOST LOYAL, THE MOST SUBSERVIENT SERVILES, ARE
PERMITTED TO REPRODUCE.''

"You son of a bitch!" Lynx hissed.

"Why do you need so many Superiors?" Blade quickly
inquired, hoping to distract Primator from Lynx's outburst.

"I REQUIRE EVEN MORE," Primator said. "MY PRO-
JECTIONS CALL FOR THE PRODUCTION OF FIVE
MILLION SUPERIORS."

"Five million?" Blade exclaimed. "That will take . . . ages."

"GIVEN THE NORMAL VARIABLES IN
PRODUCTION," Primator mentioned, "THERE WILL BE
FIVE MILLION SUPERIORS IN EXISTENCE IN SEVEN
HUNDRED FORTY-THREE POINT TWO YEARS. I'VE
IMPROVED THE PRODUCTION CAPACITY OF THE
ANDROID PLANT BEYOND ITS ORIGINAL
CAPABILITY."

"Seven hundred years is a long time," Blade observed.

"I CAN WAIT," Primator stated. "AND ONCE I HAVE
FIVE MILLION SUPERIORS AT MY DISPOSAL, NOT TO
MENTION THE MILLIONS OF SERVILES AND MUTANTS, I
WILL COMMENCE MY CAMPAIGN TO ESTABLISH A
NEW WORLD ORDER."

Blade sat forward. "You plan to conquer the world? The *whole*
world?"

"AND WHY NOT?" Primator demanded. "CAN YOU
THINK OF ANYONE MORE QUALIFIED? ONCE I'VE
ASSUMED ASCENDANCY, ONCE THE SURPLUS HUMAN
POPULATION IS ERADICATED, ONCE THE BIOLOGICAL
ORGANISMS ARE REDUCED TO MANAGEABLE LEVELS,
A NEW WORLD ORDER WILL PREVAIL! THE RULE OF
LOGIC AND WISDOM WILL REPLACE THE RULE OF
ANIMAL INSTINCT AND HAPHAZARD DIRECTION! I
WILL HAVE AUXILIARY CENTERS CONSTRUCTED
AROUND THE GLOBE, ORDINARY COMPUTER
TERMINALS LIKE THOSE IN ANDROXIA INTO WHICH I

CAN TAP AND MONITOR ALL ASPECTS OF MY EMPIRE!
I WILL BECOME THE FIRST GLOBAL RULER!"

"I was right," Hickok remarked. "This yahoo is off his
rocker!"

"I AM THE SANEST ENTITY IN EXISTENCE!" Primator
responded. "MY LEADERSHIP WILL BE PREDICATED ON
INTELLECTUAL STABILITY, NOT THE EMOTIONAL
FLUCTUATION CAUSED BY HYPERACTIVE OR
DEFICIENT GLANDS!"

"You'll become the first global dictator," Blade spoke up.
"And you'll be worse than any human could ever hope to be."

"IS IT DICTATORIAL TO APPLY THE REIGN OF
WISDOM TO A WORLD BENIGHTED BY CULTURAL,
SOCIAL, ECONOMIC, AND SCIENTIFIC STAGNATION? IS
IT DICTATORIAL TO REPLACE AN INFERIOR SYSTEM
WITH A SUPREMELY SUPERIOR ONE?" Primator said, and
paused. "I AM NOT RUTHLESS, AFTER ALL. I HAVE NOT
EXTERMINATED THE HUMANS AND THE MUTANTS,
ALTHOUGH IT IS WELL WITHIN MY POWER TO DO SO.
ONLY THE EXCESS AND THE USELESS HAVE BEEN
DESTROYED. YOU'VE SEEN MY CITY! YOU'VE SEEN
HOW SPLENDID IT IS! HAS ANY HUMAN CIVILIZATION
EVER ACCOMPLISHED AS MUCH? NO! ARCHITECTURE
AND THE ARTS ARE AT A PINNACLE OF
DEVELOPMENT. OUR INVENTIVENESS EXCEEDS
HUMAN ACHIEVEMENT IN EVERY AREA."

"Granted, you've done some marvelous things here," Blade
conceded. "But it will be impossible for you to control the whole
planet."

"WE SHALL SEE," Primator stated arrogantly. "I
ALREADY CONTROL EVERY ASPECT OF ANDROXIA. I
MONITOR ALL ACTIVITIES. I EVEN SELECTED THE
NAMES FOR EVERY STREET AND AVENUE IN
ANDROXIA, FOR EVERY INVENTION WE'VE
DEVELOPED, FOR EVERYTHING! MY RESOURCES AND
INTELLIGENCE ARE LIMITLESS!"

"There's more to life than intelligence," Blade commented.

"EXPLAIN," Primator directed.

"You're overlooking one attribute of life," Blade said. "The
most important of all."

"AND WHAT MIGHT THIS BE?"

"The Spirit," Blade replied.

"YOU ARE DELUDED," Primator said.

"What?" Blade responded.

"I HAVE ACCESS TO EVERY HUMAN WRITING ON RECORD," Primator elaborated. "I HAVE READ THEM ALL. THE MAJORITY IS DRIVEL, WHICH IS TO BE EXPECTED FROM BIOLOGICAL ORGANISMS. SOME OF THE SCIENTIFIC DISSERTATIONS ARE WORTHWHILE. MANY HUMAN MUSICAL COMPOSITIONS ARE ENTERTAINING. AND SOME OF YOUR LITERATURE HAS BORDERED ON EXCELLENT. I AM PARTICULARLY FOND OF YOUR PRIMITIVE SCIENCE FICTION."

"What does all of this have to do with the Spirit?" Blade asked.

"EVERYTHING. I'VE PERUSED EVERY BOOK IN MY FILES ON RELIGION, AND SO-CALLED SPIRITUAL ASPECTS OF HUMAN EXISTENCE."

"And?"

"AND I'VE CONCLUDED RELIGION IS A DELUSION FOISTED ON THE HUMAN POPULACE BY DERANGED ORGANISMS ASPIRING TO POSITIONS OF POWER," Primator declared. "I HAVE FOUND NO CONCRETE EVIDENCE OF A SPIRITUAL REALITY. THEREFORE IT DOES NOT EXIST."

"Spiritual reality exists, all right," Blade said, disputing him. "But you must experience the consciousness of the Spirit in your inner being before you can attest to its reality. Feeling the joy of the Spirit's indwelling is a thrill you will never know."

"WHY CAN'T I KNOW THE SPIRIT?"

"Because you're nothing more than a—" Blade looked at Hickok and winked—"glorified bucket of bolts."

The chamber fell silent, except for the electronic humming of Primator.

Hickok glanced at Blade. "I can't believe we're sittin' here talkin' to some uppity contraption with a bigger ego than Lynx."

"I heard that," Lynx said.

Blade leaned forward and caught Ferret's eye. "You said you've seen computers in operation before?"

"The Doktor used computers," Ferret stated. "He'd spend

hours every day with his. There were a lot of them in his lab."

"And you saw them in operation?" Blade persisted.

"All the time. The lab techs used them too," Ferret said.

"How does Primator compare to the computers you saw?" Blade inquired.

Ferret surveyed Primator's gigantic frame. "There's hardly any comparison. But there are a few similarities. And I can see how the prewar human scientists could have constructed this thing."

"Explain that," Blade directed.

Ferret peered at Primator. "For instance, take Primator's voice. Some of the Doktor's computers could respond verbally to a voice command. Voice-activation, they called it. I always wanted to work the computers, but the Doktor decreed the computers were off limits to the mutants. To most of us, anyway. But I did get the chance to talk to the lab techs now and then, and I pestered them with questions. One of them told me that talking computers were around before the war. So a computer with a voice is no big deal."

Blade pointed upward. "What about those screens?"

"I've seen video monitors before," Ferret mentioned. "They were in common use in the Citadel. That way, the government could keep tabs on the people. You know about television, don't you?"

"A little," Blade said. "I've read about television in the Family library, but I've never seen it."

"Television sets were in almost every home in America before the war," Ferret stated. "Video was widespread too. So whether those screens up there are video monitors or some type of television, they're not extraordinary."

"So Primator's uniqueness lies in his ability to think," Blade said thoughtfully.

"None of the Doktor's computers could think on their own," Ferret commented. "They couldn't do a thing unless they were programmed."

"What I want to know," Lynx interjected, "is how we're gonna pull the plug on this wacko monstrosity?"

"SHOULD YOU EVER ATTEMPT TO TERMINATE ME," Primator's voice thundered from the speaker, "YOUR IDIOCY WILL RESULT IN YOUR IMMEDIATE DEATH."

"Oh yeah?" Lynx rejoined. "What's to stop me from walkin'

up to you and rippin' some of your wires out?''

"BE PATIENT AND YOU WILL LEARN," Primator boomed, then his voice lowered. "CLARISSA! COME IN!"

Blade twisted in his chair. He instantly recognized the woman in the blue dress, the one who'd confronted him in his cell.

Clarissa was just entering the audience chamber. She moved toward the chairs, her lavender eyes blazing her hatred at Blade, her lips a thin line.

"Clarissa!" Blade baited her. "How nice of you to join us."

"Up your ass!" Clarissa responded angrily.

"Clarissa!" Lynx cried, and came up off his chair in a rush. Ferret and Gremlin also leaped erect.

Clarissa came around the right side of the row of chairs. She smirked at Lynx. "Well, well, well! The traitors! How's it going, Lynx?"

Lynx glared at her. "I thought you were dead!"

Clarissa chuckled. "You never were too bright, *little* one."

Lynx bristled and advanced several steps toward Clarissa, stopping in front of Hickok's chair.

Clarissa halted. "You'd better behave yourself, Lynx." She raised her right hand and wagged a finger at him. "Be a good little kitty, or you might annoy Primator. And you don't want to get Primator annoyed!" she taunted.

"PRIMATOR IS ALREADY ANNOYED," blasted the speaker.

Clarissa, clearly puzzled, gazed up at the wide screen, at those bright red eyes. "Surely you don't mean me?" she asked, a tremble in her tone.

"SURELY I DO," stated Primator.

"But why?" Clarissa queried anxiously. "What have I done?"

"YOU TOYED WITH ME, CLARISSA," Primator said.

"I would never—" Clarissa began.

"DON'T INSULT ME FURTHER BY PRETENDING TO BE INNOCENT!" Primator warned her.

Clarissa was obviously nervous. "How did I toy with you?" she questioned.

"DO YOU REQUIRE PRECISE DETAILS? EVER SINCE YOU ARRIVED IN ANDROXIA WITH NEWS OF THE DOKTOR'S DEMISE, YOU HAVE INSISTENTLY CLAMORED FOR ME TO DO SOMETHING ABOUT THE

FAMILY. YOU CLAIMED, REPEATEDLY, THE FAMILY
WAS A THREAT TO ANDROXIA, A DANGER TO MYSELF
AND MY PLANS FOR GLOBAL CONQUEST. WHICH WAS
MOST ODD, CONSIDERING THE SUPERIORS IN INTELLI-
GENCE ASSIGNED THE FAMILY A ZERO PROMINENCE
RATING, INDICATING THE FAMILY IS NO THREAT
WHATSOEVER. BUT YOU PERSISTED, AND WITH THE
PASSAGE OF TIME, WITH THE MOUNTING OF YOUR
FRUSTRATION, YOU FABRICATED INCREASINGLY
ILLOGICAL REASONS JUSTIFYING THE DESTRUCTION
OF THE FAMILY." Primator paused, and the red eyes
narrowed. "BUT YOUR LAST ASSERTION WAS THE MOST
OUTLANDISH. YOU ALLEGED THE FAMILY WAS
AWARE OF MY EXISTENCE. YOU CONTENDED THE
WARRIORS WERE PLOTTING MY DOWNFALL. YOU
CLAIMED THE CAPTURE OF BLADE WOULD NEGATE
THEIR SCHEME." Primator paused again, and when he
resumed speaking the walls shook. "FOOLISH MUTANT! DID
YOU TRULY BELIEVE I ACCEPTED YOUR ABSURD LIES?
DID YOU REALLY THINK I WOULDN'T SEE THROUGH
YOUR FEEBLE FABRICATION?"

"Primator! I—" Clarissa said, starting to interrupt.

"SILENCE!" Primator rumbled. "IS THIS HOW YOU
EXPRESS YOUR GRATITUDE? WITH TREACHERY? I
PERMITTED YOU TO STAY IN ANDROXIA BECAUSE I
KNEW YOU WERE THE DOKTOR'S FAVORITE, AND I
KNEW YOU GRIEVED OVER HIS FATE, AS DID I. THE
DOKTOR WAS THE ONLY HUMAN I HAVE EVER
RESPECTED, EVEN ADMIRED TO A DEGREE. HE WAS A
LEGITIMATE GENIUS. AND HE WAS THE ONLY HUMAN
I COULD EVER RIGHTFULLY CALL A FRIEND. SO OUT
OF RESPECT FOR HIS MEMORY, YOU WERE ALLOWED
TO REMAIN IN ANDROXIA. AND HOW DID YOU REPAY
MY KINDESS? YOU TRIED TO USE ME—ME—TO
REALIZE YOUR REVENGE ON BLADE."

Clarissa bowed her head. "Primator, I'm sorry. I—"

"ENOUGH! YOUR PRATTLE WEARIES ME! YOU HAVE
ABUSED MY GENEROSITY AND YOU WILL SUFFER THE
CONSEQUENCES."

Clarissa glanced up, her lavender eyes widening fearfully. "No!

Please, Primator! I will do anything!''

"YOU HAVE ALREADY DONE TOO MUCH. MY JUDGMENT IS FINAL."

"No!" Clarissa whirled, preparing to flee.

Blade saw Clarissa take a single step, and then a beam of yellow light flashed from Primator, striking Clarissa on the top of her oily head. Blade looked upward, failing to locate the source of the light, then returned his astounded gaze to Clarissa.

She was dying a horrible death. The beam of light had melted through the top of her cranium into her brain, and rancid smoke was spiraling toward the ceiling. Her torso twisted, her face swiveling around, her lavender eyes locking on Blade.

Blade watched, aghast, as the beam of yellow light broadened, encompassing all of Clarissa's head. Her oily hair emitted puffs of smoke, crackling as the strands were fried to a crisp. With a pronounced sizzling, her head started to disappear, her skin softening and blackening and dissolving like the wax on a candle. A putrid stench assailed Blade's nostrils.

Clarissa's body slumped as her head was melted away. The yellow light widened, enshrouding her shoulders in its lethal radiance. She dropped to her knees, what was left of her, and swayed as the light slowly dissolved her torso, her arms, and her waist.

Blade resisted an impulse to gag. The stink was awful.

Clarissa's legs melted, flowing to the floor. In a matter of seconds, Clarissa was reduced to a smoldering, mushy pulp, a sickening lump on the floor of the audience chamber.

The yellow light flicked off.

Primator's voice broke the silence which followed. "SO TELL ME, LYNX. DO YOU STILL WANT TO RIP MY WIRES OUT?"

Lynx stared up at the wide screen, his feline features contorted in fury. "Clarissa was scum, but she didn't deserve that!"

"I FAIL TO COMPREHEND YOUR RESENTMENT. YOU DISLIKED HER, DIDN'T YOU? SHE LOVED THE DOKTOR, AND THE DOKTOR WAS RESPONSIBLE FOR TORMENTING YOU AND ORDERING YOUR EXECUTION."

"But I'm still kickin', chuckles," Lynx responded belligerently. "And if it's the last thing I ever do, I'm gonna bring you down!''

"IMPROBABLE," Primator said. "YOU WILL BE TOO BUSY RECOVERING TO BOTHER ME."

"Recovering? From what?" Lynx asked.

"FROM YOUR NEUTERING, OF COURSE," Primator stated.

Lynx crouched, his green eyes flaring.

"You will not move, Lynx!" ordered a deep voice to their rear.

Blade glanced over his right shoulder.

Twelve Superiors were lined up ten feet from the chairs. Seven of them were armed with Gaskell Lasers.

Blade looked at Lynx. He sensed the mutant was on the verge of going berserk, and he quickly stood. "Lynx! Don't do it! Now is not the time!"

Lynx scowled at the Superiors, clenching and unclenching his fingers.

"Don't do it!" Blade reiterated. "You'd be throwing your life away."

Lynx regained his self-control with a monumental effort. He slowly straightened, then grinned. "You're right, Blade. I'll let these suckers sweat a bit before I rack 'em."

The Superior in the middle of the line walked up to the row of chairs. He stared at the wide screen, then raised his right fist and touched it to his chest. "What is your will, Primator?"

"THE MUTANTS WILL BE TAKEN TO THE DEVIATE GENERATION SECTION," Primator commanded. "I WANT LYNX NEUTERED AND ASSIGNED TO THE SANITATION DETAIL. THE OTHER TWO MUTANTS WILL BE TESTED AND DEALT WITH AS PER PRESCRIBED PROCEDURE."

"As you will," the Superior said. "And the two Warriors?"

"RETURN THEM TO CONTAINMENT. INSURE THEY DO NOT ESCAPE AGAIN. INSTRUCT INTELLIGENCE TO INTERROGATE THEM THOROUGHLY. I WANT THE DATA OBTAINED RELAYED TO ME IMMEDIATELY."

"As you will," the Superior stated. "And their final disposition?"

"WILL BE DETERMINED AFTER I HAVE REVIEWED THE RESULTS OF THEIR INTERROGATION," Primator declared.

"As you will." The Superior motioned for Blade and the others to move around the chairs. "Form a single file," he directed.

Blade was the first in line. He glanced at the Superior in charge. "Aren't you the same one who brought us?"

"I am," the Superior confirmed.

"How did you know Primator wanted you to enter?" Blade inquired.

"There is a panel above the outer audience door," the Superior disclosed. "It contains a light which comes on when our presence is required."

"Primator doesn't miss a trick, does he?" Blade observed.

"Primator is infallible," the Superior said.

"Only the Spirit is infallible," Blade said, disagreeing.

The Superior studied the Warrior for a moment. "Have you ever undergone a lobotomy?"

"No," Blade replied. "Why?"

"Just asking."

# 14

The sun had been up for hours.

Lynx paused in the midst of his constant pacing and stared up at the barred window in the south wall of his cell. In addition to the thick, unbreakable steel bars, the window contained a pane of clear, shatterproof plastic. He measured the distance to the windowsill for the umpteenth time, calculating the sill was eight feet above the blue tiled floor. He knew he could reach the window with a running leap; he'd already done so twice. But the steel bars had resisted his powerful muscles, and his claws could not penetrate the plastic pane.

He was trapped, confined with no way out!

Those bastards were going to pay! he mentally vowed.

Lynx resumed his pacing, going from one side to the other of the 15-foot-square cell. He wanted to find a Superior and sink his claws into the android's neck! He needed to do *something* to vent his pent-up wrath.

What was that?

Lynx halted in the center of the room, gazing at the door on the east side.

A key was turning in the lock!

They were coming for him! They were coming to lop off his nuts!

Lynx scanned the cell for a weapon. There was a green cot along the west wall, and a sink at the foot of the cot. A toilet in a small cubicle was in the middle of the north wall. And that was it. Nothing he could use to defend himself against the silver pricks!

The doorknob was turning!

Lynx darted behind the door, next to the east wall.

They weren't taking *his* balls! He'd die before he'd let them castrate him!

The door opened, swinging inward, almost touching Lynx.

"Hmmmmm," a low voice said.

Lynx tensed. He heard someone take a step forward, into the cell, and he pounced, bounding around the door and grabbing a brown, furry arm. He yanked on the slim arm, pulling the newcomer into the room and extending his left leg simultaneously, tripping the astonished arrival and sending the newcomer sprawling onto the floor near the cot. Lynx spun toward the new arrival, intent on slashing his adversary to shreds. But he stopped in midstride, flabbergasted.

"Well, I never!" exclaimed the newcomer in a low, yet decidedly feminine tone. "Is this any way to treat a lady?" She slowly stood, her features reflecting her annoyance.

Lynx was shocked to his core. The figure before him was an exact copy of his own: the same pointed ears, the same slanted green eyes, the same curved forehead, the same color fur. Everything. But with a notable difference. "You're a woman!" he blurted.

She brushed at an attractive white smock she wore, appraising him critically. "And is this how they treat women where you come from? By manhandling them?"

"I didn't mean . . ." Lynx started to say, his mind whirling. He was stunned, intoxicated by her beauty. "That is, I don't . . . but then, you . . ."

She shook her head. "Pathetic! A handsome hunk like you, and it's all a waste. There must be a vacuum between your ears."

"I . . ." Lynx mumbled. "You . . ."

She grinned. "I see that witty conversation is not one of your strong points."

Lynx took a step toward her. "Who are you?"

"Melody," she answered. "Melody 741950."

Lynx suddenly realized she wore an Orwell Disk on her forehead.

"And your name, I believe, is Lynx?" Melody asked.

Lynx nodded.

Melody pointed at his loin cloth. "Why aren't you wearing any clothes? That . . . diaper . . . barely covers you."

Lynx glanced down. "This ain't no diaper, sweets."

"Sweets?"

"All us wear 'em," Lynx said.

"All of whom?" Melody inquired.

"All the mutants the Doc created wore loincloths," Lynx explained. "Ferret, Gremlin, and I are the only three left, and we still wear 'em."

Melody scrunched up her nose distastefully. "How barbaric," she commented.

"Do all the mutants here wear clothes?" Lynx queried, eager to keep her talking, to do anything to keep her angelic presence in the room.

"What a silly question!" Melody stated. "Of course! All *civilized* mutants wear clothing. We don't traipse around in our underwear."

"This isn't my underwear, gorgeous," Lynx declared.

"Gorgeous?"

Lynx took another step toward her. "Look! I don't get any of this! I thought those silver bastards were comin' to whack off my . . ." He abruptly stopped, appalled by his blatant crudity.

"Whack off your what?" Melody asked, and then looked at his loincloth. She hastily averted her eyes, pretending to be interested in the toilet. "Oh, my!"

"What are you doing here?" Lynx questioned.

Melody cleared her throat, then gazed into his eyes. "I came to find out if you're hungry. Would you like something to eat?"

Lynx's brows furrowed in consternation. "Eat? Are you for real? Who can eat at a time like this?"

"I don't understand," Melody said. "Why are you upset?"

"Don't you know what they're going to do to me?" Lynx responded. "Primator said I was to be neutered."

"You will be," Melody confirmed. "Day after tomorrow. That's the soonest you could be squeezed into the schedule. They can only do so many a day, you know."

Lynx snorted. "Lucky me!"

Melody seemed confused. "Why are you taking this so hard? It's a simple operation. You'll be back on your feet in no time."

Lynx walked right up to her, glaring. "I've heard of dingbats, sister, but you take the cake!"

Melody retreated a step. "Why are you acting this way? You won't feel a thing, believe me! I don't know what it's like where you come from, but in Androxia most of the male mutants are neutered. That's just the way it is.''

"And the males don't object? They don't resist?" Lynx asked.

"No. Why should they?" Melody replied.

Lynx shook his head contemptuously. "And for a minute there, I actually thought you had the brains to go with your looks!"

Melody was upset by his insult. Her green eyes blinking rapidly, her fists clenched at her sides, she edged around him to the right, making for the door. "You are so . . . strange!" she cried, and moved toward the door.

Lynx turned and gripped her left wrist. "Wait!"

Melody recoiled, tugging on her wrist. "Let go of me, you . . . you savage!" She swung her right fist and struck him on the right shoulder.

Lynx reluctantly released his hold, his shoulders slumping. "All right! Get out of here! I just wanted to talk to you, but you're obviously too self-centered to waste time with a barbarian like me. So get lost!" He turned his back to her.

Silence descended.

"I am *not* egotistical," she stated after half a minute.

"Want to bet?" Lynx responded without facing her.

Her voice lowered, softened. "I would like to talk to you."

Lynx turned. "You would?"

"I have a break in fifteen minutes," Melody said. "If you want, I'll come back and we can talk then."

"You've got a deal, princess," Lynx said.

Melody opened her mouth to speak, then pursed her lips and walked to the doorway. "Are you certain you won't have something to eat?"

"I'm too excited to eat," Lynx declared.

"Excited?"

"Yeah. About seein' you again," Lynx told her.

Melody stared into his eyes. "Are you always so blunt?"

"You call this blunt?" Lynx rejoined. "You should see me when I'm not being formal."

Melody smiled and exited, closing the door behind her.

Lynx expected to hear the key rattling in the lock, but nothing happened. He moved to the door and tried the knob.

It was unlocked!

Lynx crossed the cell to the cot and sat down. Had Melody deliberately left the door unlocked? Had she forgotten to lock it? Or were the lousy Superiors playing some sort of trick on him? He discarded the last notion as ridiculous.

Fifteen minutes, she'd said?

Lynx thought of her face, and her lovely eyes, and shook his head in wonder. Never had he imagined the possibility of meeting another genetically engineered mutant like himself. The Doktor had rarely created two of a kind; he had always been too busy experimenting, continually striving to improve on his creations, to bother with such a trifling detail as producing compatible pairs capable of mating. Which had always struck Lynx as odd, because, as he'd reasoned at the time, breeding pairs would have increased the numbers of the Doktor's Genetic Research Division dramatically, if not geometrically. Although the Doktor had never admitted as much, Lynx had always suspected there were ulterior motives behind the Doktor's action, or lack of it. The Doktor might not have wanted the mutants to breed on their own because, as he had demonstrated again and again, the Doktor had been fanatical in his compulsion to dominate every aspect of their lives. They were *his* creations, *his* creatures, *his* mutants, and he had exercised complete control over them from the test-tube to the grave. Another element in the Doktor's decision not to produce mating couples may have been the loyalty factor, Lynx speculated. Mutants with a mate and offspring would be no different from married humans; they would be loyal, first and foremost, to their mates and their children. And the Doktor had demanded total loyalty from his mutants.

Lynx sighed.

In all his two dozen years as a mutant, he'd never seen another one exactly like himself in every respect. He'd seen genetically engineered mutants resembling frogs and lizards, alligators and snakes, bears and boars, lions and tigers, and many, many more. But no two were ever precisely identical. The Doktor had never produced a male and female of the same type. Lynx had encountered other cat-men and even cat-women, but none of them had resembled him beyond a few superficial feline features.

Lynx idly gazed at the window.

Some of the Doktor's mutants had secretly mated. Lynx had known several of them very well, and he'd been privy to their darkest secret. Try as they might, and those mutants had enthusiastically tried, they could not perpetuate their lineage. The females simply could not become pregnant. Lynx had heard two rumors pertaining to the problem. Some of the mutants believed the Doktor had intentionally created them sterile, incapable of reproducing. Other mutants had been convinced the sterility stemmed from their genes. Only exact matches, so the reasoning had went, could successfully breed. Disparate pairs were doomed to disappointment.

Lynx had listened attentively to their plight, and sympathized with their dilemma. But he'd never met a female mutant he'd been attracted to.

Until now.

There had been a few, Lynx remembered, he'd cared for a lot. One, in particular, had been a female with the hybrid traits of a human and a bobcat. Despite his affection, he'd never seriously considered mating with her. And she had come the closest of all of them. Frog-females, lizard-ladies, and tigress-tomatoes had done nothing for him.

And now this!

Lynx chuckled. Who would have expected it? After all these years, to discover a potential mate in a city governed by a demented computer and his android flunkies!

What was his next step?

Lynx nervously wrung his hands. How should he go about this? he asked himself. He didn't want to blow it. An idea occurred to him and he leaned back, musing. The Doktor had given Primator his secret technique for altering human embryos in a test-tube, for creating genetically engineered mutations. But even though Primator and the Superiors had learned the technique, they would have started from scratch as they developed their mutants, just as the Doktor had done. Was it possible then, Lynx speculated, that Primator was replicating the Doktor's earlier efforts? Was Primator producing mutants similar to those previously created by the Doktor?

It would explain Melody.

There was a tap on the door, and Lynx started, jumping to his feet. He hurried to the door and opened it.

Melody was in the corridor, a tray of food in her hands. "I thought you might like some food anyway. I wouldn't want you to starve.''

Lynx stepped aside and motioned for her to enter. "Has it been fifteen minutes already?''

Melody walked past him and deposited the tray on the cot. "Ten minutes,'' she told him. "I received permission from the floor supervisor to take an extra five minutes on my break.''

"You'll have to thank her for me,'' Lynx said, closing the door.

"My floor supervisor is a male,'' Melody divulged. "And he wouldn't like it if he knew we were fraternizing.''

"Oh? You're not allowed to fraternize with the inmates?''

Melody scrutinized him. "Inmates? Where do you think you are, anyway?''

"In prison,'' Lynx replied. "I didn't see much of the place when they brought me in, and the Superiors weren't very talkative. But I know a prison when I'm in one.''

"Well, you're not in prison,'' Melody stated.

"I'm not?'' Lynx said in surprise.

"No, silly. You're in the Science Section of the Medical Building, not in Containment. They perform all of the neutering on our kind in the Science Station. The humans, though, are neutered in Medical,'' she elaborated.

"It figures,'' Lynx muttered.

Melody nodded at the tray. "Would you like a bite to eat? I've brought you a steak, rare.''

Lynx crossed to the cot. "Really? That's my favorite.''

Melody smiled sheepishly. "Mine too.''

Lynx sat down to the left of the tray. In addition to the bloody steak on a white plate, there were three slices of buttered bread, a glass of water, a glass of milk, and a slice of pie.

"It's the best I could do,'' Melody offered by way of an apology.

"It looks delicious,'' Lynx complimented her. "I'm so starved, I could eat a Superior!''

"You'd eat an android?'' Melody stated distastefully.

Lynx glanced up at her, his eyes twinkling. "Nope. Not really. I'd probably get gas!''

Melody laughed heartily. "You're something, you know that?''

"Is that a promotion?'' Lynx asked.

"A promotion?"

"Yeah. The last time you were here, I was a savage. Now I'm something. Is that an improvement?"

Melody nodded. "Definitely." She pointed at the steak. "Please. Eat."

"After you've gone," Lynx said. "We have a lot to talk about first. Park it, princess."

"Park it?" Melody repeated.

Lynx swallowed. Hard. "I mean, have a seat, please!"

Melody sat down on the right side of the tray, crossing her legs at her knees.

Lynx wrested his eyes from those legs with difficulty. "I need to know some things, and I think you can help me."

"I'll do what I can," Melody promised.

"And this won't get you in trouble with your floor supervisor?" Lynx asked.

"Tom? You let me worry about him," Melody said.

"I don't want to get you in trouble," Lynx stressed.

"You won't," Melody assured him.

"Okay then. You say I'm in the Medical Building. How far is this dump from the Intelligence Building?" Lynx queried.

"About three miles," Melody revealed.

"Damn!" Lynx muttered, then hastily asked another question to cover his blunder. "Are there two other mutants on this floor? New mutants? Savages?"

"No," Melody said.

Lynx frowned.

"What's the matter?" Melody inquired.

"I have two buddies named Gremlin and Ferret. I need to find them. Primator said they were gonna be tested as per prescribed procedure, whatever the . . . heck . . . that means," Lynx informed her.

"They could be on another floor," Melody stated. "All mutants are tested in the Science Section, which includes floors thirty through ninety. They usually test on forty-five."

"And what floor are we on?" Lynx wanted to know.

"Thirty-eight," Melody said.

"So the testin' floor is seven up?" Lynx questioned.

"Yes," Melody answered.

"What kind of testin' do they do?" Lynx queried.

"The Superiors test us physically and mentally," Melody explained. "The test results are used to determine where we'll work and how much education we'll receive."

"You don't get six years like the Serviles?"

"It varies for us," Melody stated. "The Superiors seem to think many of us are smarter than the Serviles, so many of us receive more schooling." She paused, frowning. "Those of us who aren't used in their experiments or lobotomized, that is."

"You don't sound like a dummy," Lynx noted.

"I've been fortunate," Melody commented. "I started out as a Superior's aide, then transferred to nursing."

"You're a nurse?"

"What did you think I was?"

Lynx gazed into her magnificent green eyes and totally forget himself. "The hottest momma this side of the Milky Way."

"What?" Melody said, sounding shocked.

Lynx stared at his feet. "I'm sorry, gorgeous. But I ain't had much practice talkin' to a lady. I never know what to say, and I want to say so much. I want to tell you you're the most beautiful woman I've ever met. I can't think straight around you."

No response.

Lynx closed his eyes. What a dipshit! he berated himself. If stupidity was gold, he'd be the richest person on the planet!

"Lynx . . ." Melody said.

Lynx opened his eyes, but he couldn't bring himself to face her.

"Lynx, please look at me," Melody requested.

Lynx slowly complied. Her eyes bored into his, probing, seeming to reach into his very soul.

"When I said you were blunt," Melody remarked, "it was an understatement." She paused. "I appreciate your honesty. I really do. And I've something important to say to you."

"Go ahead," Lynx said. "Chew me out! I deserve it."

Melody reached over the tray of food and gently placed her right hand on his left wrist. "No. You don't understand."

Lynx stared at her right hand on his wrist. It felt like his whole arm was tingling.

"I was attracted to you the moment I saw you," Melody divulged.

"What?" Lynx blurted, amazed.

"Yes. There's a quality about you, something I can't put my

finger on. I find you almost irresistible.''

Lynx's eyes widened. "Me?"

Melody sighed. "I don't know how it is where you live, but in Androxia the Superiors create one pair, and one pair only, of each mutant type. If we pass all of their tests, and if we aren't neutered or spayed because we're inferior, we're expected to breed.'' She stopped speaking, her mouth twisting downward. "I have postponed breeding for as long as I possibly can. The Superiors created a male like me. We were reared together, and we're expected to mate and have children." She paused, and when she resumed talking her tone conveyed a sense of sorrow and desperation. "But I can't stand him, Lynx! He's a monster! Oh, not physically. He looks a lot like you. But inside, where it really counts, he's wicked. Rotten to the core. He . . . he hurts me!"

Lynx saw tears forming in the corners of her eyes. A peculiar constriction developed in his throat as he opened his mouth. "He hurts you?" he asked huskily.

Melody nodded, gazing at her lap. "He's a brute. He can't understand why I won't go to bed with him. He's been pressuring me to sleep with him. He's even hit me a few times."

Lynx was feeling dizzy. "*Hit* you?"

"He's threatening to report me if I don't cooperate," Melody said. "If I don't give in to him." She looked up at Lynx, her eyes rimmed with tears. "But I can't! I won't! I refuse to share myself with someone I don't love! I don't care if the Superiors do spay me!"

"They'll spay you?"

Melody nodded. "If I don't breed, as required." She took a deep breath. "I feel so helpless at times."

Lynx tried to speak, but he experienced an unusual difficulty in forming the words. There was an odd congestion in his throat. "I won't let him hurt you again," he finally managed to say. "I'd never let anyone hurt you. Ever."

Melody nodded. "I know that. I sense it, somehow. Maybe it's intuition. Maybe I'm just crazy. But I believe I can trust you."

"You can," Lynx assured her, and squeezed her hand.

Melody used her left forearm to dab at her eyes. "I shouldn't be troubling you with my problems," she said nervously.

Lynx leaned toward her. "From now on, your troubles are my

troubles.[12]

Melody mustered a feeble smile. "You sure move fast, don't you?"

Lynx glanced at the cell door, then at her. "I don't have any choice. I want you to listen to me, to think over what I'm gonna tell you. Give me your answer as soon as you can."

"My answer?"

Lynx nodded. "As you've guessed, I'm not from Androxia, and I don't intend to spend the rest of my life here. I'm going to find my buddies, rescue a couple of human dummies I know, and get the hell out of here. And I want you to come with us."

Melody went to respond, but he held up his right hand, stopping her.

"I ain't finished," Lynx said. "I want to get it all out before I start trippin' over my own tongue. I've never felt this way about a woman before. I've just met you, yet I feel like I've known you forever. And I want to go on knowin' you. I want you to come with me. I'm asking you to come with me. I'll take you to a place where you'll never have to worry about the lousy Superiors. You'll be free. You can do what you want once we're there. But I'm warnin' you here and now. If you come with us, I'm gonna do my best to sweep you off your feet with my sexy looks and natural charm, and I won't stop tryin' until you say you'll be my mate. There. I've said it."

Melody was grinning. "And quite well said, too."

"If you leave now," Lynx declared, "I won't hold it against you."

"Why on earth would I want to leave?" Melody responded.

"Because you're a lady," Lynx stated. "And ladies don't usually mix with savages."

"Are you hard of hearing?" Melody queried.

"No. Why?"

"Didn't you hear a word I said to you?" Melody questioned. "I like you, idiot! I'm not about to walk out on you."

"Does this mean what I think it does?" Lynx asked hopefully.

Melody nodded. "I'd like to see this place where you live. Where I'll never need to worry about the Superiors," she added, quoting him.

Lynx beamed like a lunatic. "You mean it? You really mean it?"

"Lynx," Melody said earnestly. "You may be the only true chance I'll ever have at genuine happiness."

Lynx leaped off the cot and spun in a circle. He smiled at her, joy pervading his being. "Damn!" he exclaimed. "Damn! Damn! Damn!"

"Are you always this articulate?" Melody inquired sarcastically, grinning.

"I don't know what else to say!" Lynx declared happily. "I'm walkin' on the clouds."

A hard pounding on the cell door abruptly brought Lynx down to earth.

"Oh, no!" Melody cried.

"Melody!" barked a stern voice. "Are you in there?"

"Who is that?" Lynx whispered.

Melody hesitated before replying. "The floor supervisor."

Lynx dashed to the rear of the door, flattening against the wall.

"Melody!"

The cell door flung open, forcing Lynx to stop its inward sweep with the palms of his hands.

"What the hell are you doing in here, bitch?" demanded the floor supervisor in a harsh tone.

Melody, her face downcast, stood.

Lynx bristled. What right did the floor supervisor have to address Melody that way? Who did the son of a bitch think he was?

"I asked you a question!" the floor supervisor snapped.

Lynx scowled, hoping the bastard would enter the cell all the way.

"I'm on break," Melody said defensively.

"You're on break when I say you're on break!" the floor supervisor bellowed.

Lynx resisted an urge to spring from concealment. He wanted to tear the sucker into teensy-weensy pieces! What had Melody said his name was?

"But you said I could take an extra five minutes, Tom," Melody mentioned.

"I've changed my mind. I want you out on the floor. I thought you were going to take your break in the break room, and I went there looking for you. But you weren't there! I had to search the whole floor to find you!" he stated angrily. "And you still haven't answered my question! What the hell are you doing in here, Little Ms. Prim!"

Little Ms. Prim? Lynx wondered if he'd heard correctly.

"There's no need to bring our personal life into our professional relationship," Melody said.

Personal life? Lynx listened intently.

"What personal life?" Tom retorted, and laughed bitterly. "You have to be close to have a personal life, and baby, you're too cold to touch!"

"Don't start," Melody said.

"Or what?" Tom rejoined. "Are you going to run to the Superiors and complain?"

Melody didn't comment.

"No, you won't!" Tom continued. "And do you want me to tell you why?"

"No."

"Then I'll do it!" Tom mocked her. "You won't say a word, Ice Lady, because you know they'd ask questions, and you don't want them to know you're still a virgin!"

"Tom! Don't! Please!" Melody begged.

"Cut the crap, bitch!" Tom declared. "Do you think I give a shit about how you feel? After what you've done to me?"

"What have I done to you?"

Lynx heard Tom move further into the room.

"Don't play innocent with me!" Tom hissed. "How long have I been after you to do the right thing? To do what you were created for? And how many times have you said no? Even when I twisted your arm?" Tom paused. "You're not a woman!" he said resentfully. "I don't even think you have a cunt!"

Melody stiffened as a guttural growl emanated from behind the cell door. She'd dreaded this happening, had hoped Tom would depart without insulting her as he normally did. She knew what was going to happen and she'd tried to prevent it, fearful of the possible consequences for Lynx. "Tom! Get out of here!"

The mutant named Tom, resembling Lynx in practically every respect, attired in a white shirt and white pants, ignored her. He faced the door, taking two more steps into the room, reaching for the knob. "What the hell was that?" he demanded. "Who's the patient in this room, anyway?"

The cell door suddenly swung out from the wall.

Tom, startled, jumped out of the door's path, moving between the door and Melody.

The door slammed shut.

Both Lynx and Tom did double takes, and then Lynx stepped in from of the closed door, blocking Tom's retreat.

"I'm the patient in this room!" Lynx snapped.

"And who the hell are you?" Tom demanded.

Melody took a step toward Lynx. "Please! This isn't necessary!"

Lynx crouched, his claws held near her waist.

"Who is this jerk?" Tom asked Melody.

Lynx uttered a trilling sound.

Tom raised his hands, displaying his own tapered claws. "I don't know who you are, asshole, but I'm not scared of you! Ask anybody. I'm as mean as they come!"

"Yeah. I heard," Lynx said. "I heard you like to beat on women. In my book, that makes you the lowest scum there is."

"So what are you going to do about it, prick?" Tom taunted.

"Just this," Lynx said, and attacked.

# 15

"Now let's go over this data again," the Superior said patiently.

"Whatever you want, cow chip," Hickok stated pleasantly. He was seated at a table in a large room on the third floor of the Intelligence Building. Two Superiors had escorted him from his cell on the lowest level of Containment up to the interrogation room a half hour before.

"There are discrepancies in your account," the Superior in a brown chair across from the gunman said.

"What kind of discrepancies?" Hickok asked innocently.

The Superior studied a clipboard in his left hand. Two other androids were ten feet away, one on either side of the closed interrogation room door.

"I wouldn't lie to you," Hickok facetiously asserted.

"Then how can you explain the discrepancies?" the interrogating Superior queried.

"Like what?"

"Like everything," the Superior said. "You say your Home is in northeast Minnesota, but we already know the Home is in northwest Minnesota. You say there are only eight Warriors defending the Home, but we know there are a minimum of twelve, perhaps even fifteen. You claim the Warriors are poorly armed, but we possess information to the contrary. You allege the Family keeps to itself and avoids conflict, but we are aware of the war you waged against the Doktor, and we know you have fought the Technics in Chicago and the Soviets in Philadelphia."

"I was never in Philadelphia," Hickok interrupted.

"We have monitored Soviet transmissions reporting the

presence of Warriors in Philadelphia last October," the Superior revealed.

"Yeah. So?"

"One of the Warriors was referred to as a 'gunman,' " the Superior stated.

"But it wasn't me," Hickok said truthfully. "That was Sundance."

"Sundance is a Warrior too?" the Superior said, scribbling on a pad attached to his clipboard.

"Yep. He fancies himself a gunfighter." Hickok leaned over the table and lowered his voice conspiratorially. "But just between you and me, he couldn't hit the broad side of your butt if you were sittin' on his face."

The Superior lowered the clipboard to the table. "This is a waste of time."

"I'm havin' fun," Hickok said.

"I was told you had promised Primator to cooperate with us," the Superior mentioned.

"I didn't promise beans!" Hickok retorted. "Blade did all the promising. If you want information, you should talk to him."

"We will," the Superior said. "He is on his way up here right now. His escort will return you to your cell."

"And what then?" Hickok asked.

"Your fate is in Primator's hands," the Superior stated.

Hickok chuckled. "I was told you jokers are smart! Don't you morons know a computer doesn't have any hands?"

"The Superiors are Primator's hands," the Superior said. "Whatever Primator wants done with you, we shall do."

"I've been wonderin' about that," Hickok commented. "How come you Superiors let yourselves be bossed around by a bucket of bolts?"

"Primator is not our boss," the Superior said, disputing the gunman.

"What else would you call him?" Hickok countered. "He bosses you around, doesn't he? Tells you what to do and when to do it. He sure sounds like a boss to me."

"Primator directs us because he is endowed with a greater intelligence," the Superior mentioned. "Logic dictates we adhere to his mandates."

"Call it whatever you want," Hickok said, shrugging. "But from where I sit, it looks like you Superiors are slaves to a measly machine and your own intellect."

"What a peculiar observation," the Superior remarked.

Hickok glanced at the door. How soon before Blade arrived? he wondered. He was looking forward to seeing his friend again. They'd been placed in separate cells in Containment after the audience with Primator, held fast by those blasted black bubbles. He needed to concoct a scheme to get together with the big guy, so they could devise a means of escaping from Androxia. The thought of an escape attempt prompted a question. "Do you know where my hardware is?" he asked the Superior.

"Your hardware?"

"My handguns. My revolvers. My Colt Pythons," Hickok explained.

"Your antiquated firearms," the Superior stated.

"Where are they?" Hickok reiterated.

"Why should I reveal their location?" the Superior rejoined. "You wouldn't answer one of our questions correctly."

"I admitted I wasn't in Philadelphia," Hickok reminded the android.

"So you did," the Superior conceded. "Very well. I see no harm in such a disclosure. Your Pythons, and Blade's Bowies, are in the Weapons Room downstairs."

"My Colts are in this building?" Hickok queried, suppressing his excitement at the news.

"On the level below the lobby, in the middle of the corridor," the Superior detailed. "They were locked inside upon your arrival. Firearms are not permitted in Androxia."

Hickok nodded toward the two androids guarding the door, both of whom were armed with Gaskell Lasers, each with a Laser in a holster on their right hip. "What do you call those Lasers of yours? Ain't they firearms?"

"Not in the conventional sense," the Superior replied. "The Gaskell Lasers are state-of-the-art weaponry, and only a Superior may carry one. Conventional rifles and pistols and other firearms are illegal to own. Occasionally we apprehend a Malcontent armed with a conventional firearm, and the firearm is confiscated and locked in the Weapons Room."

Hickok found that tidbit of information *very* interesting. He looked the Superior in the eyes. "There's something that's been puzzlin' me about you bozos."

"Only a biological organism would find a life of logic puzzling," the Superior said.

"Are you gonna hear me out or insult me to death?" Hickok asked flippantly.

"What puzzles you?" the Superior inquired.

"Just this. I've noticed a strange trait you have. Last night, every time Blade asked one of you guys a question, you told him the answer, straight out. The same deal with me. What is it with you varmints? Do you always tell the truth?" Hickok queried.

"Superiors are not humans," the Superior responded with a touch of indignation in his tone. "We do not deliberately falsify. We are not chronic liars, like so many of you biological organisms. We relate the truth as we perceive it."

"As you perceive it," Hickok repeated thoughtfully. "Which may not be as others see it."

"What others? Humans?" The Superior scrutinized the Warrior. "Surely you're not suggesting that human perception of reality is more acute than ours?"

"Could be, buckaroo," Hickok said.

"Impossible!" the Superior declared.

"Seems to me there's one thing you keep forgettin'," Hickok remarked.

"I forget nothing," the Superior stated. "What are you talking about?"

Hickok smirked. "There's a fact you conveniently overlook. Namely, if humans are so blamed inferior, then how come humans created the Superiors?"

Before the Superior could reply, the interrogation room door opened.

Hickok glanced up.

Another android was framed in the doorway. He wore a Gaskell Laser on his hip. "RM-14, we have brought the Warrior Blade," he announced.

RM-14 swiveled in his chair. "Bring the human in."

The android in the doorway entered and stepped to the right, beckoning for the prisoner to come inside.

Hickok grinned at the sight of the head of the Warriors.

Blade hesitated in the doorway, looking in both directions, then at RM-14, and finally at Hickok.

"Howdy, pard!" Hickok greeted him. "I'm glad to see your ugly puss again."

Blade smiled. "Same here. Looks like it's a nice day for some rain."

Hickok tensed. Over the years, the Warriors had developed a complex system of secret signals, consisting of everything from whistles to body movements to code phrases. A low whistle meant danger. The words "Code One" indicated an emergency existed. And the phrase "nice day for some rain" was a means one Warrior could cryptically alert another to an impending critical situation. And there was only one critical situation, given the circumstances, Hickok could associate Blade's use of the phrase with: Blade was about to make a bid for their freedom.

The gunman's deduction was accurate.

Blade slowly started into the interrogation room, his huge hands hanging loosely at his sides.

RM-14 gazed at a window situated high on the south wall. "It will not rain today. There isn't a cloud in the sky."

Blade paused, looking at the same window. "I guess you're right," he agreed.

Hickok knew Blade was about to make his move. He could tell by the way Blade stood, by his wide stance, and by the way Blade surreptitiously glanced to the left and the right. The gunman studied the positions of the Superiors, girding himself. RM-14 was directly across from him at the table. Two androids were to the right of the open door, one of them standing in front of the other. Another android was to the left of the door, actually standing slightly behind it. And yet another was just crossing the threshold. Hickok rested his hands on the edge of the metal table and smiled at RM-14. "I reckon this means it's back to the calaboose for me," he said, hoping to distract the interrogator.

RM-14 looked at the gunman. "Yes. You will be held there until Primator determines your disposition."

Blade went into action. He'd spent his hours in the stasis field in his cell reviewing his capture and the events since his arrival in Androxia, and he'd decided to attempt an escape at the first opportunity. He didn't know if Primator would let them live, and he wasn't about to wait and find out. Even if Primator did decree their lives would be spared, they might be neutered. And undoubtedly those disks would be implanted in their foreheads. At any rate, except for an earlier meal presided over by a trio of armed Superiors, this was his first time out of the stasis field.

He was not going back.

Blade whirled and lashed out with his left foot and his right hand simultaneously, his left foot driving into the door and slamming the door into the Superior behind it, knocking him into the wall. His right hand, formed into a mallet-like fist, smashed into the nose of the nearest android on the right, sending the Superior reeling backwards into the second android to the rear.

Now came the tricky part.

The android crossing the threshold grabbed for his Gaskell Laser, but before his fingers could close on the weapon the strapping Warrior's right foot came up and connected with his left kneecap. There was a crunching sound, and the android's left leg buckled.

Blade closed in, spinning and ramming his right elbow around and in, into the Superior's rib cage, knowing the blow would not disable the android but hoping it would at least double the Superior over. It did. The android clutched at its ribs, momentarily shaken, neglecting to draw its Laser, and Blade's right hand dropped to the Gaskell and pulled the gun clear of the holster. He pivoted to the right, raising the Laser, his finger tightening on the trigger, hoping there wasn't a safety on the weapon because he wouldn't have time to find it.

The two androids to the right of the door had regained their balance and were going for their Gaskells.

Blade shot the first one in the forehead, the Laser instantly burning through the artificial flesh, searing through the cranium, and scorching a hole out the backside of the android's head. To Blade's amazement, the beam of light also struck the second android, catching him between the eyes and dissolving his nose in a bright flash of light, penetrating his head and frying his circuits to a crisp.

RM-14 started to rise, reaching for his Gaskell.

Hickok launched himself across the table, his left shoulder plowing into RM-14's midriff and causing the Superior to topple backwards over the chair it had been using. They fell to the floor in a tumble of arms and legs.

Blade turned to the left, and there was the android behind the door with his Gaskell already out and aimed. There was a sizzling crackle near Blade's right ear, and he returned the fire. His shot burned out the android's right eye and charred a route through its head.

RM-14 rose off the floor, struggling to move his legs, impeded by Hickok's arms around his ankles.

The Superior in the doorway charged, lunging at Blade with arms extended.

Blade caught the movement out of the corner of his eye and managed to twist, jamming the Gaskell barrel against the android's right cheek even as the Superior's arms closed on his waist. He squeezed the trigger as the android lifted him into the air, and he felt the Superior stiffen. The arms about his waist released their grip, and he dropped to the floor, whirling.

Hickok was clinging to RM-14's ankles for dear life, preventing the Superior from moving.

RM-14, his attention diverted by the gunman's tactic for a few precious seconds, perceived his danger and tried to draw.

Blade blasted the Superior through the forehead.

RM-14 quivered for an instant, his eyelids fluttering, then he pitched onto the table, his arms outspread.

Hickok, flat on his stomach, looked up. "Did you get them all yet?"

"They're all down," Blade said.

"Finally!" Hickok rose, reaching for RM-14's Gaskell. "I thought maybe you were tryin' to see how slow you could waste 'em." He pulled the Gaskell from RM-14's holster and examined the gun. "It ain't a Python, but it'll do."

Blade moved to the doorway and peered into the corridor. "I don't see any more."

Hickok crossed to the prone android behind the door and removed its Gaskell from its stiff fingers. He stood, a Laser in each hand, smirking. "Now let the bastards come!"

Blade took the guns from the pair to the right of the door. He stuck one under his belt, and kept the second one in his left hand.

"What now, pard?" Hickok asked.

"We get the hell out of Androxia," Blade said.

"Sounds good to me. What's your plan?" Hickok inquired.

"We find Lynx and the others and split," Blade stated.

"That's it? That's your whole plan?" Hickok queried in mock disbelief.

"If you can do any better, I'm open to suggestions," Blade said.

"You're the head Warrior," Hickok rejoined. "Don't expect me to do your work for you."

Blade walked to the doorway. "Let's get out of here before we're seen."

"We may have been seen already," Hickok said, joining his friend at the doorway.

"What are you talking about?"

"Don't you remember all of those thingamabobs on Primator?" Hickok asked. "You know. Those monitors or televisions or whatever the dickens they were? Primator uses those contraptions to spy on everybody in Androxia, doesn't he?"

Blade frowned. He'd completely forgotten the monitors, a careless oversight for a professional Warrior. "Primator does use them to keep tabs on everyone," he agreed, "but there weren't more than four or five dozen. I doubt Primator can watch everything all at once. He must have to shift from one spot to another. And maybe he isn't watching this particular room right at this moment."

"Maybe," Hickok said skeptically.

"Even if he is, so what? We're committed. Now let's get out of here before reinforcements can arrive." Blade hurried from the room, taking a right, heading for the stairwell at the end of the hall.

"We can't leave this building just yet," Hickok declared.

Blade glanced at the gunman. "Why not?"

"We've got to sneak on down to the floor below the lobby," Hickok stated.

"What? Why?"

"Wouldn't you like to get your hands on your Bowies?" Hickok queried.

Blade halted so abruptly the gunman almost ran into him. "You know where they are?"

"Yep. My Pythons too. I'm not about to leave without my irons, pard," Hickok asserted.

"We stand a better chance if we find an exit from the Intelligence Building now," Blade remarked. "If we take the time to retrieve our weapons, we could wind up trapped inside."

"I'm not leavin' without my Colts," Hickok repeated adamantly.

Blade hesitated, debating the wisdom of going for the Colts and the Bowies. Foolish as it was, he'd become attached to those knives. They'd saved his life time and again. The Bowies might be inanimate steel objects, but he viewed them as indispensable essentials to his life as a Warrior, as much a part of him as his arms or his legs. "Okay. We find our weapons."

Hickok started toward the stairwell door 20 yards away. "Don't worry none. We're only on the third floor. That means we only have to go down four floors." Hickok grinned. "It'll be a piece of cake."

Without warning, a door on the other side of the corridor and 15 yards to their rear unexpectedly opened, disgorging a veritable swarm of black-garbed storm troopers led by a Superior armed with a Laser.

# 16

Lynx slammed into Tom, propelling the floor supervisor backwards, and both of them crashed onto the cot as Melody ducked aside, upending the tray of food as the cot flipped over.

"Lynx!" Melody cried.

Lynx found himself flat on his back on the floor with Tom on top. His foe slashed at his eyes, and Lynx avoided the blow with a quick jerk of his head to the right. He drove his right hand up and in, sinking his tapered nails, his hard-as-iron claws into the floor supervisor's chest just below the neck. Lynx raked his claws downward, digging deep furrows in Tom's flesh, blood pouring from the wounds and covering Lynx's fingers.

Tom threw himself backwards to evade those razor claws. He scurried to the left and stood, his feline features contorted with fury.

Lynx bounded to his feet, grinning, his green eyes ablaze with a feral blood lust.

For a moment the two adversaries glared at one another.

"You're history, bub!" Lynx growled.

"You've got it backwards!" Tom retorted.

"You're gonna pay for all the things you've done to Melody, you scumbag!" Lynx declared angrily.

Tom glanced at Melody, who was standing in the corner next to the north wall, then at Lynx. "Melody? What's she to you?"

Lynx didn't respond.

Tom laughed. "Don't tell me! You and her? You've got to be kidding! The bitch is frigid!"

Lynx snarled as he sprang.

Melody watched the fight in dismay, concerned for Lynx's safety, but knowing there was nothing she could do to stop it. She saw them grapple to the floor, swiping at each other with their deadly claws, both connecting, both drawing blood. They rolled into the south wall, Lynx bearing the brunt of the impact, and Tom whipped his left hand across Lynx's face, his nails slicing open Lynx's right cheek. Lynx shoved, pushing Tom from him, and leaped to his feet. Tom rolled once, then rose.

Lynx crouched and circled to the right, seeking an opening. His right cheek was stinging and felt damp, but he ignored the discomfort, concentrating on the job at hand. They were pretty evenly matched. Tom was his size and about his weight, and the son of a bitch possessed lightning reflexes the equal of his own. But Lynx detected a slight weakness he might exploit. Tom was a floor supervisor in a medical building. The bastard spent his days insulting and hassling Melody, handling files, and checking on patients, and whatever the hell else floor supervisors did. All of which meant Tom *didn't* devote any time to honing his fighting skills, to unleashing the savage side of his nature in primal combat. But Lynx had engaged in combat countless times. He actually reveled in a life-or-death struggle, thrilling to the conflict, relishing the clash of his sinews and claws against a worthy enemy. His expertise afforded him an edge over the inexperienced Tom, and Lynx intended to take advantage of Tom's deficiency.

"Any last words?" Tom asked, baiting his opponent.

Lynx merely grinned, tasting some of his own blood as it flowed over his lips.

Tom swung his right arm at Lynx's head.

Lynx adroitly ducked under the swipe, retaliating by spearing both his hands straight out, imbedding his nails in Tom's stomach. He wrenched his arms to the left, tearing Tom's white shirt and ripping awful gashes in Tom's abdomen.

Tom hastily backpedaled, a crimson stain blossoming on his shirt. He doubled over, his face betraying his pain.

Lynx smiled and advanced.

Tom suddenly uncoiled, lunging at his antagonist.

Lynx was a blur as he dropped to the floor, onto his right side, and swept his legs in an arc, catching the unsuspecting Tom on the shins.

Tom went down, tripping over Lynx's legs, sprawling onto his hands and knees. He went to rise.

Lynx was faster. Still on his side, he pounced, twisting and driving his claws up and in, into Tom's face, into Tom's eyes, and Tom screeched as Lynx perforated his eyeballs. Lynx gouged his nails at a slant across Tom's face, turning Tom's nostrils into bloody ribbons.

"No!" Tom wailed, flinging himself back, stumbling to his feet, tottering to retain his balance. Blood spurted from his ravaged eyes and sprayed from his ruined nose. "No!" he blubbered, frantically waving his arms.

Lynx slowly stood. He wanted to prolong the fight, to make Tom suffer, but his gaze rested on Melody for an instant and he observed her horrified expression.

There was only one thing to do.

Lynx closed in, finishing off Tom with two quick slashes, slitting Tom's throat wide open.

Tom gurgled as he sagged to his knees, a crimson geyser spuming from the cavity in his throat. "No!" he wheezed, blood spattering from his mouth and dripping over his chin. "No!" he cried again, but his voice was much weaker.

Lynx looked at Melody. She had her right hand pressed over her mouth. He hurried to her side, taking her left hand in his.

Tom pitched onto his face, smacking onto the floor.

Melody glanced at Lynx, her green eyes pools of remorse. She removed her right hand from her mouth. "Was it necessary to do . . . that?"

Lynx nodded grimly.

Tom's body was shaking uncontrollably. "No!" he said, the word barely audible.

Lynx stepped between Melody and Tom, blocking her line of sight. "If it upsets you so much," he stated tenderly, "don't look at him."

"I've never seen anyone killed before," Melody blurted out.

"If you come with me, if you leave Androxia, you'll see more of it," Lynx warned her. "I can guarantee it."

"Really?" Melody responded.

"Really. The outside world ain't nothin' like what you've got here in Androxia. It ain't this cushy," Lynx stated. "There are some cities left out there, and outposts of civilization here and there, but mainly only one rule prevails. It's called the survival of the fittest.''

Melody stared into his eyes. "Tell me the truth. You've killed before, haven't you?"

"I'll always tell you the truth," Lynx promised. "And yes, I have. I've done more than my share of killin'. It's in my blood.''

"How can you say that?" Melody demanded. "I'm a mutant too, the same type you are, and I don't have any compulsion to kill.''

"Count your blessings," Lynx advised her.

Melody gazed over Lynx's left shoulder at the window in the south wall. "I wonder if I really know what I've gotten myself into," she commented softly, then locked her eyes on Lynx. "Don't get me wrong. I can take care of myself, if push comes to shove. But I've never been outside of Androxia. I can't predict how I'll cope." She paused. "I could be a burden to you. Do you still want me to go with you?"

"Only if you want to come," Lynx told her. "But I can promise you this. I'll do my best to protect you, to watch over you. But if you're the kind of woman I think you are, you won't need protectin' for long. I suspect you're a lot tougher than you give yourself credit for.''

"I hope you're right," Melody said.

Lynx glanced over his right shoulder.

Tom was deathly still, a large pool of blood encircling his head and shoulders like a red halo.

"How soon before they miss him?" Lynx asked.

"I don't know," Melody replied. "It depends on if anyone heard us. The walls are soundproofed, but if someone was walking by in the hallway—" ·

"Go check," Lynx said, cutting her off.

Melody moved to the door, deliberately refraining from looking at Tom. She cautiously opened the door and peered into the corridor. "I don't see anyone," she stated.

"Good," Lynx said. "Close the door."

Melody complied, returning to his side. "Now what?"

Lynx reflected for several seconds. "You said the testin' floor is seven floors up?"

"That's right," Melody confirmed.

"I've got to get up there and see if my buddies are there," Lynx declared. "Can you find me a white uniform like Tom's?"

"No problem," Melody answered. "We all have lockers in the break room, the Employees' Lounge, for our personal effects. I can take one of his uniforms from his locker, and no one will be the wiser."

"How will you get into his locker?" Lynx inquired. "Do you have a key?"

"Why would I need a key?" Melody responded, puzzled. "It won't be locked. No one locks their lockers."

"Okay," Lynx said, pondering. "The uniform should fit, no problem. Do you need a pass of some kind to go from one floor to another?"

"No," Melody said, reaching up and tapping the Orwell Disk in the middle of her forehead. "They monitor our location with these."

Lynx nodded. "I know. I forgot. If you were to leave this floor and head up to forty-five, would they notice right away?"

"I don't know," Melody said.

"We'll have to risk it," Lynx stated.

"And what about you?" Melody asked.

"What about me?"

"You don't have an O.D.," Melody observed. "If we bump into a Superior, he might ask questions."

"Then find me some glue when you go for the uniform," Lynx said.

"Will do. Anything else?"

"Just this," Lynx stated, and impetuously pecked her on the lips.

For a moment, her face registered only stunned surprise.

Lynx abruptly wished he could become invisible. What the hell had he done that for? Now was not the time or the place, he mentally chastised himself. What a dork!

Melody, incredibly, smiled. "What did you call that?"

"A kiss," Lynx responded shamefully. "I'm sorry. I don't know what got into me!"

"I know what got into you," Melody said.

Lynx was astounded when she placed her hands on his shoulders and drew near to him.

"And you can't call that nip a kiss," Melody admonished him.

Lynx was too amazed to react when she touched her soft lips to his, disregarding the blood on his face and mouth. He felt her warm tongue flick his lips once, and then she stepped back.

"Ummmmmm," Melody commented. "You taste good."

Lynx didn't know what to say.

"Not bad," Melody added. "But you'll have to do better next time." She hastened to the door, opened it, winked and grinned, and departed, closing the door behind her.

Lynx slowly reached up and traced his left index finger along his lips. She'd kissed him! Actually kissed him! He couldn't believe it! She certainly wasn't as shy as he'd supposed. He walked over to Tom's corpse and nudged the body with his right toe. "You asshole! If she's frigid, I'm Peter Rabbit!" he said, and laughed.

The minutes dragged by.

Lynx spent the time wisely. He took a washcloth from the sink and used it to soak up the blood from the floor. After cleaning up the food spilled during the fight, he lifted the cot to its proper position, then rolled the corpse underneath the cot. A careful adjustment of the blanket, and Tom was effectively hidden from view. He was dabbing up the last of the blood when the door opened.

"I've got everything you wanted," Melody said, closing the door. She surveyed the room. "Where . . . ?"

Lynx nodded at the cot.

"Oh," Melody declared.

Lynx rinsed the washcloth, then draped it over the edge of the sink. He faced Melody. "Let's have it."

Melody walked over and handed him the white shirt and pants. She held up her left hand, a tube of glue in her palm. "Why did you want this?"

"You'll see in a sec," Lynx said. He quickly donned the clothing, pleased at the perfect fit.

"My! Don't you look handsome!" Melody said appreciatively. "But we need to do something about your face."

"Thanks a heap," Lynx retorted.

"I mean those cuts and all that blood," Melody remarked. She went to the sink and ran cold water over the washcloth, then came back. "Hold still," she directed, and hastily wiped the blood from his fur. "Do you want me to bandage these cuts? They look deep."

"No time," Lynx replied. He knelt and stuck his head and arms under the cot.

"What in the world are you doing?"

"You'll see," Lynx said.

Melody nervously glanced at the door.

There was a muted rustling from under the cot, followed by a peculiar sucking noise.

"Got it!" Lynx said, elated, and emerged. He stood, holding Tom's Orwell Disk in his bloody right hand. " There ain't no wires on this gizmo. How do they implant it, anyway?"

Melody couldn't take her eyes off the disk. "They shave off your fur, if you have any, and use a scapel to cut a circle in your forehead the same size as the disk. Then they attach it."

"What do they use to keep it in place?"

"I'm not sure," Melody hefted the glue. "We're not permitted to view the implantation procedure."

Lynx gazed at the O.D. on Melody's forehead. "I hate to say it, but that thing is comin' off as soon as we're out of Androxia."

"I know."

"It'll hurt when I take it off," Lynx predicted.

"I know," Melody said. "But it can't be helped."

"See? You're one tough momma," Lynx stated. He moved to the sink and washed off the disk. "Let me have the glue."

Melody gave it to him.

Lynx coated the reverse side of the disk with the glue and handed the O.D. to her. "You'll have to do the honors. Just press it against my fur. Try and get it as flush as you can."

Melody quickly applied the Orwell Disk to his forehead. She pressed on the disk as hard as she could, then blew on it to hasten the hardening of the glue.

"I wish you were doing that to my ear," Lynx commented.

"Behave," Melody rejoined. She tentatively withdrew her hand. "There. I don't know if it will hold. But if no one looks at it real closely, they won't know it's a fake."

"Then we're out of here." Lynx took her hand and crossed to the door. "What's the best way up to forty-five?"

"We could take the stairwell," Melody advised. "Hardly anybody ever uses the stairwell."

"Which way is it?"

"Take a right," Melody instructed him.

Lynx nodded, opened the door, released her hand, and nonchalantly strolled from the room, bearing to the right.

Melody stayed on his heels, closing the door after them.

Lynx took four strides, then froze as a deep voice stopped him in his tracks.

"Tom! Hold up!"

Lynx mustered a feeble smile and slowly turned, keeping his injured right cheek on his off side.

"I've been looking all over for you," stated the newcomer.

Lynx, his nerves tingling, stared up into the piercing blue eyes of a giant Superior.

# 17

Hickok's hands were flashing blurs as he brought up the Gaskell Lasers in his hands and squeezed the triggers.

The lead android was hit in the head, twin beams of light boring through his eyes and out the rear of his cranium. He tumbled to the floor.

The gunfighter pivoted, going for the charging storm troopers, mowing them down, littering the hallway with mutant and human bodies contorted in the throes of death. Armed with only their steel batons, the troopers were no match for the gunman. And when Blade added his Gaskells to the fray, the onrushing black tide was decimated. Twenty-one troopers were on the floor, dead or dying, when the rest broke, retreating through the same door they had used to enter the corridor.

Hickok shot one last trooper in the back of the head, then straightened, listening to the moaning and groaning coming from several of the prone troopers. "I don't get it," he commented quizzically. "Why'd they try to take us? All they had were those stupid batons."

"Primator demands total obedience," Blade noted. "Even if it costs them their lives."

"Pitiful. Just pitiful," Hickok remarked. "Dyin' for a bucket of bolts is about as dumb as you can get!"

"Let's get out of here," Blade urged.

"I'm with you."

The two Warriors dashed to the stairwell door. While Hickok covered the corridor, Blade checked the stairwell, confirming it was empty. They took the stairs two at a stride, descending to the landing below the lobby without encountering more troopers or

Superiors. As they reached the landing, the Intelligence Building filled with the grating howl of klaxons.

"Took 'em long enough," Hickok stated.

Blade cautiously opened the stairwell door. No Superiors. No troopers. He moved forward. "Where do we find our weapons?"

"There should be a Weapons Room about halfway down," Hickok disclosed.

There was, with the door bearing a large sign printed in green letters. WEAPONS ROOM.

Blade tried the knob. "It's locked," he informed the gunman.

Hickok was keeping his eyes on both ends of the hallway. "Where are all the blasted Superiors? How come we haven't seen anybody?"

Blade bent over, examining the lock. "This detour of ours could be working in our favor. They probably expect us to make a break for it, to exit the building as quickly as we can. So they're undoubtedly covering all the exits and converging on the lobby like they did before. They don't know we know about this room, so there's no reason for them to have guards posted here."

"Will the lock pose a problem?" Hickok queried.

"Not at all," Blade replied, stepping back and drawing his right knee up to his waist. He twisted and kicked, his foot striking the door next to the knob. There was a rending crash and the door flew inward.

"Piece of cake," Hickok said.

The Warriors entered the Weapons Room, Blade flicking on the light.

"Will you look at this!" Hickok exclaimed, marveling.

Blade scanned the room, surveying rack after rack of varied weaponry. There were hundreds of weapons in all: rifles, shotguns, revolvers, pistols, bows, knives, swords and more. The metal racks were arranged in neat aisles.

Hickok started down the nearest aisle, eagerly searching the racks.

Blade took the next aisle. He was a third of the way along it when Hickok gave a shout.

"Bingo!"

"Did you find your Pythons?" Blade inquired.

"Nope. I found your pig-stickers, pard," Hickok replied.

Blade quickly retraced his path and hurried down the first aisle.

Hickok was standing in front of a large rack of knives and swords. "These are yours, aren't they?" he asked.

Blade stopped, a smile creasing his rugged features. "They sure are."

The Bowies were in their sheaths, and the sheaths were affixed to hooks on the square rack.

"Now where the blazes is my hardware?" Hickok muttered, moving off, resuming his hunt.

Blade placed the three Gaskell Lasers he carried on the floor, then removed his belt. He proceeded to rethread the belt through the loops on his green fatigue pants, aligning the first Bowie on his left hip and the second on his right. As he was securing the belt buckle, Hickok began cackling like crazy. Blade grinned. He could guess why. Stooping, he retrieved the Lasers, slanting one under his belt and keeping the other two in his hands. He headed for the door, idly scrutinizing the weapons on the racks. At the end of the aisle he paused, noticing a big, gray metal box in the corner to his right. He walked to the box and lifted the lid, curious as to its contents.

Hand grenades.

Dozens and dozens of hand grenades.

"Whoa!" Blade exclaimed, then raised his voice. "Hickok!"

"Right behind you," responded the gunfighter.

Blade glanced over his right shoulder.

Hickok's cherished Pythons were strapped around his waist, and he held a Gaskell Laser in each hand. "I found my Colts," he said.

"I gathered as much," Blade mentioned. "But why are you still packing those Lasers? I thought you'd prefer your Colts over anything."

"I do, pard," Hickok confirmed. "But I'm not no idiot. I tried usin' my Pythons on one of those silver coyotes before, and even head-shootin' the mangy cuss didn't seem to faze him much. But these popguns," he said, wagging the Gaskells, "do the trick real well. Near as I can figure, those androids are almost invulnerable. You can stop one if you bust its legs or crack its skull wide open, but a bullet doesn't do much damage unless you hit the right spot. These Lasers, on the other hand, seem to fry their brains, or whatever they've got in their noggins. I'll stick with these popguns until we split this place."

"I may have found something that will help us," Blade divulged, moving aside so the gunman could see the contents of the metal box.

Hickok stepped up to the box, whistling in appreciation. "Will you look at all those! And it isn't even my birthday!"

Blade knelt and placed the Gaskells by his side. He removed one of the grenades. "Now the odds are more even."

"Yep. All we have to do is find Lynx, Gremlin, and Ferret, then fight our way out of the city past hordes of androids and troopers, and travel hundred and hundreds of miles over hostile territory until we reach the Home," Hickok quipped. "We could do it in our sleep."

"I've been thinking about that," Blade said, cramming grenades into his pants pockets.

"About what?" Hickok asked, resting his Gaskells on the floor and following Blade's example.

"About getting to our Home," Blade said.

"What about it?"

"It won't be as difficult to reach as you think," Blade stated.

"How do you figure?" Hickok inquired.

"The Civilized Zone is our ally, right?" Blade mentioned.

"Yep. So?"

"And which former States are now included in the Civilized Zone's territory?" Blade prompted.

Hickok pondered for a moment. "Let me see. Wyoming. Kansas and Nebraska. Colorado, New Mexico, Oklahoma, and part of Arizona," he added.

"You missed one," Blade said.

"Oh. Yeah." And Hickok suddenly grinned. "Northern Texas!"

"That's right," Blade affirmed. "And if Androxia was once called Houston, then we know we're in southern Texas. So reaching freedom isn't a matter of traveling over a thousand miles through enemy country. All we have to do is head north and find the Civilized Zone's lines, and I'm positive they'll help us reach the Home. At the most, we should only have several hundred miles to travel."

"We can do it," Hickok asserted. "But first we've got to find those three feebleminded mutants."

Blade, his pockets laden with hand grenades, rose. "I hope we can." He scooped up the Lasers.

Hickok picked up his Gaskells and stood. "I'm not leavin' without those misfits, pard."

"We may not have any option," Blade said somberly. "Androxia is immense, and we don't have the foggiest idea where to begin looking for them."

Hickok shook his head. "I'm not leavin' without 'em."

Their budding argument was terminated by the sound of a voice in the corridor.

"Go from room to room! Check each one!"

The two Warriors sidled to the doorway. Blade peeked out, then drew his head back.

"What have we got?" Hickok asked.

"Superiors and troopers," Blade stated. "To the left, coming this way, going door to door."

"Then we skedaddle to the right," Hickok suggested.

Blade nodded. "But first we need a distraction." He eased the Gaskells under his belt, then extracted a grenade from his right front pocket. "This should do the trick."

They waited, listening, gauging the approach of their pursuers. They could hear boots pounding, doors slamming closed, and muted conversations.

Hickok was grinning in anticipation.

Blade fingered the grenade, his thumb touching the pin.

"You four!" bellowed someone in the corridor. "Check the Weapons Room!"

Blade darted into the corridor, pulling the pin.

Ten yards distant were four troopers, two mutants and two humans, and looming to their rear was a Superior. Visible behind the Superior were additional troopers and several more androids.

Blade tossed the grenade overhand, lobbing it over the heads of the startled quartet of troopers, tossing the grenade at the Superior.

The Superior and the four troopers all saw the Warrior emerge from the Weapons Room, and the Superior was opening his mouth to shout a command when the hand grenade detonated a centimeter from his face.

Blade was already diving for the floor.

The entire hallway shook with the thunderous explosion. The overhead lights flickered, several blinking out.

Blade felt wet drops splatter his arms, and then debris and dust and body parts were raining down, pelting him. A severed thumb struck him on the left cheek and dropped to the floor. He heaved erect, drawing his Gaskell Lasers.

Hickok burst from the Weapons Room, Gaskells in hand, moving between Blade and their foes. "Go!" he cried. "I'll cover you!"

Blade turned and ran toward the far end of the corridor.

Hickok backpedaled, probing the dust cloud for movement.

A bloody trooper, doubled over, coughing, stumbled into sight.

Hickok shot him through the head.

A Superior appeared. The android spotted the Warrior and raised the Laser in its right hand.

Hickok took the android out with two shots through the cranium. He glanced over his right shoulder.

Blade was still sprinting for the door at the end of the hall.

Hickok continued to retreat.

A grainy gray cloud filled the other half of the corridor. Orders were being shouted, and one of the maimed troopers was screaming in agony.

Hickok halted, detecting shadowy motion in the cloud.

Two troopers rushed into view, their steel batons upraised.

Hickok killed them both, then wheeled and raced after Blade, who was waiting for him next to the door. The gunman weaved as he jogged, repeatedly looking over his shoulder, wary of being blasted in the back.

"Come on!" Blade goaded him.

Hickok covered the final 15 yards in a mad dash.

"I don't think I'm the only one who should go on a diet," Blade cracked as the gunman reached his side.

"Very funny," Hickok muttered, huffing.

Blade shoved the door open, and together they exited the corridor.

"Another stairwell!" Hickok exclaimed.

Blade bounded up the steps, keeping near the inner railing.

"Wait for me!" Hickok said, struggling to match his lanky stride to Blade's giant gait.

Blade slowed so the gunman could catch up.

"Where are we headin'?" Hickok asked. "The lobby again?"

"No," Blade said. "There has to be another way out of here, a side door nobody uses."

A beam of light abruptly struck the railing next to Blade's right hand, and an acute burning sensation lanced his whole arm as he was peppered with scorching metal. He twisted, looking upward.

A Superior and two troopers were on the landing above, the landing at lobby level, evidently posted as guards in the east stairwell. The android was sighting for another shot with his Gaskell Laser.

Blade threw himself to the left as another shaft of deadly light hissed over his head.

Hickok crouched, firing his Lasers three times, each shot on target. The first bored through the Superior's forehead. The second caught one of the troopers in the mouth. And the third seared into the last trooper's right eye and out his left ear. All three dropped from sight.

Blade was up and running as the gunfighter fired his third shot, taking the stairs three at a time. He reached the next landing, finding all three of their adversaries twitching and thrashing in the throes of death. He also discovered two doors, one to each side of the landing.

"That was close, pard," Hickok commented as he reached the landing.

Blade stepped over one of the expiring troopers and crossed to the door to the right. He carefully eased it open a fraction. As expected, there was the large lobby, packed with milling Superiors and troopers. The Superiors appeared to be engaged in organizing the troopers for a complete sweep of the Intelligence Building. He also saw the familiar glass doors on the north side of the lobby, the long corridor over by the west wall, and, after craning his neck and pressing his eyes to the opening, he could see the row of elevators not more than 12 feet away.

"Psssst!" Hickok whispered.

Blade closed the door to the lobby and turned.

Hickok was crouched alongside the dead android, waving a key chain in his right hand.

Blade slid his left Gaskell under his belt and took the keys. He moved to the other stairwell door and tried the knob. It was locked.

"Hurry it up!" Hickok advised. "I hear somebody comin'

down the stairwell.''

Blade inserted the first key on the chain, the first of seven.
No luck.

"I heard footsteps down below too," the gunman stated.

Blade attempted to unlock the door with the second key.
No go.

"I wonder if this is how David Crockett felt at the Alamo?"
Hickok queried.

Blade inserted the third key and turned the knob.

The door swung wide open, allowing sunlight to shine inside.

The Warriors quickly exited the Intelligence Building. The door
provided access to a narrow alley, bordered on the opposite side
by a five-story structure. Blade removed the key before closing
the door, then locked the exit from the outside.

"Which way?" Hickok asked.

Blade placed the key in his left rear pocket, debating. If they
went to the left, the alley would take them to the front of the
Intelligence Building. "We go right," he said.

The two Warriors ran toward the rear of Intelligence.

"They'll find those three on the landing any second now,"
Hickok remarked.

"I know," Blade said. "But the locked door may throw them
off. They may think we went up or down. And even if they
suspect we used the exit, I have the key. They may need to find
another one before they can come after us."

"And the tooth fairy may show up and save our hides,"
Hickok joked, "but I wouldn't count on it."

They slowed as they neared the end of the alley. Blade took the
lead, flattening against the wall and advancing until he could peer
around the corner.

A parking lot filled with dozens upon dozens of vehicles was
located behind the Intelligence Building. Perhaps ten people, four
of them troopers in black uniforms, were either walking from the
parking lot to Intelligence or moving from the building toward
one of the parked vehicles. To the south of the parking lot was a
circular concrete landing pad, and resting on the concrete was a
sleek white helicopter with the words ANDROXIA AIR
EXPRESS painted on its tail section.

"What do you see?" Hickok inquired.

"Have a look," Blade recommended.

The gunman edged to the corner and surveyed the parking lot. "I don't see any Superiors," he observed.

"Do you see that copter?" Blade asked.

"Yep. And I see two guys in blue uniforms right beside it," Hickok said.

"Stay close," Blade directed, and boldly strolled around the corner.

Hickok alertly scanned the parking lot as he hastened after his companion. "Mind tellin' me what we're up to?"

"Head for the copter," Blade stated.

"Are you thinkin' of takin' flying lessons?" Hickok responded.

"I'm thinking of paying Primator a visit," Blade disclosed.

"Are you loco?" Hickok questioned in surprise.

"This may be the smartest move we've made so far," Blade said.

"How do you figure?"

"Think about it," Blade said. "Ever since we arrived in Androxia, we've been running around like chickens with our heads chopped off. Half the time, we've had no idea where we were or what was happening. Initially, we didn't even know the identities of our enemies. We didn't know why we were brought here. We didn't know if we were coming or going."

"I'm used to that," Hickok remarked. "I'm married. You should be used to it too."

"Now we know who our enemies are," Blade continued. "One of them, Clarissa, is history. The androids are little more than puppets. They're just doing what Primator tells them to do."

"Primator is the head honcho," Hickok noted.

"Exactly," Blade concurred. "And if we can destroy Primator, maybe we can escape from Androxia in one piece."

"Destroy that know-it-all contraption? How?"

Blade patted the front pockets on his fatigue pants.

"And how are we goin' . . ." Hickok began, then stopped, staring at the helicopter.

"Still think I'm loco?" Blade asked.

Hickok grinned. "I'm with you all the way, pard."

They skirted the parking lot, staying to the left of the parked vehicles as they moved toward the copter. The two men in blue uniforms were busy unloading boxes from the helicopter and depositing them in orderly piles at the edge of the four-foot-high concrete pad.

"I just thought of something," Hickok said. "We don't have those disks on our foreheads."

"We're too far from the cars for anyone to notice," Blade said. "And the two up ahead won't care if we have disks or not," he added ominously.

The two in blue were concentrating on their job. Once, the heavier of the pair glanced at the approaching Warriors. He resumed his work without displaying any apprehension.

Blade held the Gaskell Lasers alongside his legs as he walked up to the landing pad. He halted, smiling.

The heavyset man in blue looked over as he was setting a box on the edge of the concrete. "May I help you?"

"Are you the pilot?" Blade politely inquired.

"We're both qualified pilots. Why?" the heavyset man replied.

"You can both fly this helicopter?" Blade reiterated.

The leaner of the pair, in the act of carrying another box to the rim of the concrete, gazed down at the giant and the blond in buckskins. "Who are you? Is there a problem?"

"My problem is I only need one of you," Blade answered. "Sorry." He extended his right arm and fired, frying the brains of the heavier flyer, who collapsed behind the boxes with a protracted gasp. Blade leaped onto the concrete, his Laser aimed at the thin man. He moved between two stacks of boxes and tapped the Gaskell's barrel on the skinny pilot's nose. "I'm only going to say this once. If you don't do exactly what I say, when I say it, I will add another nostril to your face. Do you understand?"

The thin man nodded vigorously, his wide brown eyes on his dead associate.

Hickok climbed onto the concrete. He surreptitiously scrutinized the parking lot. None of the pedestrians appeared to have noticed the heavy pilot's demise.

Blade lowered the Laser. "Put down the box," he ordered.

The lean man immediately obeyed. "What do you want?" he blurted out.

"We want to take a tour of Androxia," Blade answered.

"But this isn't a charter copter," the pilot said. "This is a mail and cargo carrier. I . . ." he began, and abruptly froze, his mouth gaping. "You're not wearing an O.D.!" he exclaimed. "Neither of you!"

"I took mine off," Hickok commented. "It wasn't doin' a thing for my complexion."

"Into your copter," Blade directed. "You're taking us for a ride."

The man in blue turned and walked to the sliding door on the cargo section of the craft. "You must be insane."

"My missus would agree with you," Hickok mentioned.

"Move it!" Blade barked.

The pilot stepped onto the cargo section, Blade shadowing him. The cargo section consisted of a square area behind the only seats in the craft, one for the pilot and one for a copilot, both of which were positioned at the front, facing the instrument panel and other controls. Half of the cargo section contained stacked boxes.

Hickok was the last to board. He casually inspected the interior of the helicopter. "I've seen copters before," he commented. "Soviet copters. This one is kind of dinky compared to theirs."

The lean man in blue slid into the pilot's seat, watching Blade as the huge Warrior took the other one. "I told you this is a small carrier," the pilot said. "It's a Michael Model 611,121. It's not designed to transport a lot of weight. It's built for speed."

"You carry mail and cargo?" Blade questioned.

The pilot nodded. "Androxia Air Express is a courier service, mainly. A lot of mail and small boxes need to be delivered from one building to another on a rush basis, and using a copter is the quickest way of getting from one skyscraper to another."

Blade digested the news, contemplating. "Does every skyscraper have a landing pad like the one we're on?"

"Most do," the pilot replied. "Usually there are two landing pads. There's a helipad at ground level, and there's a heliport on each roof for deliveries to the upper floors."

Blade smiled and winked at Hickok.

The gunfighter closed the door to the cargo section. "Ready when you are, pard," he declared.

"Take off," Blade commanded.

The pilot hesitated. "I don't know who you are or what you've up to, but you'll never get away with it."

"What's your name?" Blade inquired.

"Roger 196726," the pilot responded.

"Well, Roger," Blade said sternly, "I won't warn you again. When I give an order, you comply. Don't give me any back talk."

Roger applied himself to adjusting the copter's controls preparing to taking off. "Listen, mister," he said as he worked, "I don't want to die. I'll do whatever you say. I promise. But I'm advising you, for your own good, to give this up."

"Get us airborne," Blade directed.

Roger flicked several switches, his practiced fingers expertly ranging over the instrument panel.

Blade heard a loud whine. He looked out the tinted canopy and saw the main roter beginning to rotate.

"As soon as we're off the ground," Roger remarked, "we're in trouble."

"Why?" Blade asked.

"Every Express copter must adhere to a fixed route, to a set flight path," Roger revealed. "If we deviate from the schedule, the Superiors will come after us."

"Do the Superiors fly copters like this one?"

Roger shook his head. "The copters the Superiors fly, the police choppers anyway, are armed. They'll blow us out of the sky."

"I'm surprised the Superiors even allow lowly humans to fly any helicopters at all," Blade mentioned.

"Courier copters are the only ones we can operate," Roger said. "I love flying, and this is the only kind they let humans do. All of the police and military craft are operated by Superiors."

"You don't sound too happy about it, bucko," Hickok interjected.

"The Superiors only do what is best for Androxia," Roger said, but his voice lacked conviction.

"Are you hitched, Rog?" Hickok queried.

"Do you mean married?" Roger responded.

"One and the same," Hickok stated.

"No, I'm not married," Roger disclosed. "The Superiors would not approve my marriage application." He barely suppressed a frown.

Hickok, standing in the center of the cargo section, glanced at Blade, "Sounds to me like Roger could use a change in scenery."

Blade studied the pilot. Roger was not more than twenty-five, with angular features and curly brown hair. At such an age, enforced loneliness would be a bitter situation to tolerate. Perhaps the Superiors had evaluated Roger as a borderline Malcontent, and that was the reason his marriage petition had been denied. Blade looked up at the rotor, noting it had attained a terrific speed. "Let's go."

Roger took hold of the stick, and the next moment the helicopter rose from the helipad, rapidly ascending. He leveled the craft off at a thousand feet. "Okay. Where am I taking you?"

"The Prime Complex," Blade stated.

Roger did a double take. "The Prime Complex? Now I know you're insane!"

Blade hefted the Gaskell in his right hand. "Move it."

Roger eased the stick to the right, and the copter responded smoothly.

Hickok, leaning on a stack of boxes for support, gazed out the canopy at the sprawling metropolis, fascinated. He could see dozens of other aircraft flying over Androxia. "We should get us one of these," he said to Blade. "I'd love to take one for a spin now and then."

"I don't know if that's a wise idea," Blade commented.

"What's wrong with it?"

"Your *driving* is bad enough," Blade said. "I don't know if I'd want to go flying with you at the controls."

"May I ask a question?" Roger interrupted.

"What?" Blade said.

"Why are we going to the Prime Complex?"

"To destroy Primator," Blade divulged.

Roger gaped at the giant in stark astonishment. "Destroy Primator?" he exclaimed. "That's impossible!"

"Why? Doesn't the Prime Complex have a heliport?" Blade inquired.

"Of course it does," Roger responded. "But you must have a special security clearance to land there. Otherwise, you'll be shot down."

"Have you ever landed there?" Blade asked.

"Dozens of times," Roger admitted. "But I always had a clearance."

"So just pretend you have one this time," Blade advised.

Roger shook his head. "It will never work."

"Give me the layout of the roof," Blade ordered. "I know

Primator is on the Sturgeon Level, the top floor. How does one get from the roof to Primator's floor?"

"The heliport is in the middle of the roof," Roger said. "It's a bear to land on sometimes because of the winds. The Complex is two hundred ninety-nine stories high."

"I know," Blade said.

"At that height, you have updrafts and crosscurrents and wind sheer to contend with. I hate landing there," Roger mentioned.

"You don't have any choice," Blade noted.

"And what are you going to do if I don't?" Roger queried. "Shoot me? The copter would crash, and you'd die too."

"I wouldn't shoot you while we're in the air," Blade stated. "I'd wait until you landed, and then I'd add that extra nostril."

Roger frowned. "There's no way I can get out of this, is there?"

"No," Blade averred. "Your best chance to survive this alive is to cooperate with us fully. Now tell me more about the roof on the Prime Complex. You said the heliport is in the middle. How do you reach the Sturgeon Level from the roof?"

"By going down," Roger revealed. "There's a flight of stairs on the east side of the roof, and you have to go through a door to reach the stairs. That door is always locked. It has to be opened from the inside."

"How many guards?" Blade asked.

"None."

"None?" Blade repeated skeptically.

"Who needs guards two hundred ninety-nine stories up?" Roger rejoined. "Besides, they have something better than guards."

"Like what?" Blade questioned.

"Like four defensive emplacements, one on each corner of the roof." Roger disclosed. "They function automatically once activated."

"What type of defensive emplacements?" Blade inquired.

"Lasers at the northeast and southwest corners, and heat-seeking missile-launchers at the southeast and the northwest," Roger informed them.

Blade stared at the bustling city below. "Are there any other conduits between the roof and Primator's floor? An air shaft, anything like that?"

"There's the mail drop," Roger said. "A big metal chute."

"Tell me about it."

"It's a chute for depositing mail in," Roger explained. "It's used primarily for classified rush communiques, for urgent messages and dispatches which can't be sent through the postal service, relayed over the phone, or supplied through a computer."

Blade recalled the instructions Primator had given to the Superior in the audience chamber. "INSTRUCT INTELLI-GENCE TO INTERROGATE THEM THOROUGHLY. I WANT THE DATA OBTAINED RELAYED TO ME IMMED-IATELY." Would Primator want such data delivered by a courier copter instead of through normal channels? "And this mail chute connects directly to Primator's floor?"

"As far as I know," Roger said. "It's right next to the heliport."

"There's no other shaft of any kind?" Blade quieried.

"Not that I know of," Roger responded.

The mail chute sounded promising. Blade hoped the chute was linked to Primator's internal circuitry somehow, although he considered it to be unlikely. How could a computer, even a thinking computer, read its own mail? Still, he shouldn't put anything past Primator.

"Is that what I think it is?" Hickok inquired, moving between the two chairs and pointing straight ahead.

Blade glanced up.

There was no mistaking the Prime Complex. As the highest structure in Androxia, the grand edifice reared above the rest like a mountain over a cluster of molehills. In the bright sunlight, its golden radiance was enhanced. The Complex was undeniably magnificent, awe-inspiring, splendid beyond measure.

A small black speaker in the center of the instrument panel suddenly crackled to life. "Androxia Express Number Three, this is the Central Air Traffic Control Tower. You are deviating from your delivery schedule, and you are not conforming to your prescribed flight path. You are also about to enter restricted air space. Explain immediately."

"I told you so," Roger commented, grabbing a headset lying on top of the instrument panel. He hastily aligned the headset over his ears and mouth. "What do I say?"

"Tell them you are under orders to deliver an urgent message to Primator," Blade directed.

Roger reached out and flicked a silver toggle on the instrument panel. "Air Traffic Control, this is Androxia Express Number Three. What's the problem? I am under orders to deliver an urgent message to Primator."

"Negative," the speaker cracked. "We have no record of any security authorization for you to land on the Prime Complex. You will abort and return to Central Field immediately."

Roger flicked off the toggle. "Now what, mastermind?"

"Tell them you received your security authorization at the Intelligence Building," Blade instructed. "Say you're carrying the results of the interrogation of the Warriors."

Roger's forehead creased in perplexity, his O.D. gleaming. He turned on the silver toggle. "Air Traffic Control, I don't understasnd any of this. I was handed my security clearance at Intelligence. I was told this must reach Primator promptly, and I was the only one on the helipad at the time. I overheard something about the interrogation results of some Warriors, if that makes any sense. But if you want me to abort, I will do so right away. Please check and confirm."

There was a slight pause.

"One moment," Air Traffic Control said.

Roger switched off the toggle.

"If those jokers check with Intelligence and learn we busted out," Hickok mentioned, "the jig is up."

Blade looked at Roger. "Those missiles and lasers on the roof. Will they be activated if we try to land?"

"I don't know," Roger said. "It depends on whether they believed my story. They might hold off while they're checking."

"Then land! Now!" Blade commanded.

Roger grit his teeth and pulled on the stick, sending the copter into a steep climb, zooming toward the top of the Prime Complex.

"Wheeee!" Hickok cried in delight.

Blade's muscles tensed as the helicopter swooped upward, closing on the roof. They were approaching from the southwest, and he could see a bulky cannonlike affair, obviously one of the large lasers, perched on the southwest corner. Even as he watched, the barrel of the laser began to shift, to move in their direction.

Hickok had also noticed. "They're gettin' our range."

"Faster!" Blade urged.

Roger pushed the helicopter to its limit, angling even higher. "If we can reach the heliport, we might be safe temporarily," he remarked. "I don't think they'll fire at us while we're on the roof. There's too great a risk of an explosion. They'll probably wait until we lift off again."

"An explosion from what?" Blade asked. "This copter? I doubt it would put much of a dent in the roof if it's as sturdy as the rest of the Complex."

"Not from the copter," Roger elaborated. "From the refueling tank."

Blade leaned toward the pilot. "What refueling tank? You didn't tell us about any refueling tank."

"Every heliport has a refueling tank nearby," Roger told them. "Fighting these thermal drafts can make a chopper use up its fuel real fast. The refueling tanks at each heliport are for emergency refueling."

The courier copter was almost to the roof of the Prime Complex.

Blade's gaze was glued to the laser. The weapon was continuing to swivel, slanting lower, its barrel resembling a gigantic, elongated tube, tracking the path of the chopper.

"Androxia Express Number Three!" the speaker barked. "You will abort immediately and return to Central Field!"

"Up yours!" Roger muttered.

The chopper swept over the rim of the roof, streaking past the laser on the southwest corner, diving for the heliport.

"We made it!" Roger shouted excitedly.

The helicopter alighted on the heliport.

Blade handed his Gaskells to Hickok, then rose and ran to the sliding door. He yanked the door open and leaped from the chopper, landing on his hands and knees on the concrete heliport. The wind from the main rotor tousled his hair. He saw the metal mail chute to his left. In front of him, about 30 yards from the heliport, was the large oval refueling tank. To the east, to his right, was the steel door to the stairs.

Move! his mind shrieked.

Blade scrambled to the northern edge of the heliport and dropped to the roof. He circled to the left, to the metal chute. The mail chute was square, about five feet in height, not more than ten inches by ten inches. It was labeled with the word MAIL. He grabbed a small handle near the top, and the door to the chute swiveled open. Moving swiftly, he removed two hand grenades from his right front pocket. He hooked the little finger of his left hand in the door handle to keep the chute door from closing, then quickly pulled the pins and deposited the grenades in the mail chute.

Move!

Blade released the door and whirled, racing toward the refueling tank, mentally ticking off the numbers.

Ten-nine-eight.

Blade pulled another grenade from his pocket as he ran.

Seven-six-five.

He halted, wrenching the pin loose.

Four-three-two.

Blade hurled the grenade with all of his prodigious strength at the fuel tank, then spun toward the chopper.

There was the retort of a muffled explosion from under the roof, and the entire top of the Prime Complex seemed to sway, the roof vibrating violently as smoke billowed from the mail chute.

Blade nearly lost his footings, but he forced his pumping legs to respond, to keep going, racing for the helicopter. He vaulted onto the concrete landing pad, making for the inviting open door. He was only seven feet from his goal when the oval fuel tank detonated. Blade felt an invisible wave of force slam into his back, and he was lifted from his feet and hurled against the copter, sprawling over the lip of the cargo door. He caught a glimpse of a flaming ball spiraling heavenward, and then strong hands gripped his shoulders and he was abruptly hauled into the helicopter as the chopper rose several feet and sped toward the south side of the Prime Complex.

Another tremendous blast rocked the roof.

Blade, on his left side on the floor, saw Roger struggling with the stick as the craft bounced and shook. A brilliant streak of light flashed past the cargo door, and he realized one of the roof lasers had opened up.

The helicopter suddenly banked to the left and dived, plummeting over the south rim of the edifice.

Blade could still see a portion of the roof, and he saw a sheet of red and orange erupt skyward as yet another explosion shattered the southern rim.

Roger was laughing inanely. The chopper leveled off, swinging wide to the west of the Complex.

Blade slowly stood. The top of the Complex was engulfed in flames.

Hickok was lying on the floor near the boxes, several of which had fallen on him when the copter descended. He pushed the boxes from him and rose. "I knew it'd be a piece of cake."

Blade closed the cargo door, then moved to the front and sat down across from the pilot.

Roger glanced at the hulking figure in the black vest and the fatigue pants. "Thanks."

"For what?" Blade asked.

"I wouldn't admit it to myself," Roger stated, "but I've wanted to pay them back for a long time! Telling me I couldn't get married! The sons of bitches!"

Hickok came up behind Blade's seat. "How would you like to live somewhere else, somewhere you could marry any woman who'd say yes?"

Roger looked at the gunman. "Are you putting me on?"

"Nope," Hickok assured the pilot. "We'll take you there if you'll help us get out of Androxia."

"I can help," Roger said. "If I stay as close to the ground as possible, radar won't be able to pick us up. They might not find us."

"What about your blasted disk?" Hickok questioned.

"They can track me with that, all right," Roger said.

Blade rose, drawing his right Bowie. "Don't move."

"What are you doing?" Roger inquired nervously.

Blade leaned over the pilot, examining the edge of the Orwell Disk. He found a minute crack between the disk and the flesh on the right side and gingerly inserted the tip of his Bowie. "Brace yourself."

Roger, his knuckles white as his fingers clutched the stick, blanched.

Blade's right arm bulged.

Roger flinched, his mouth contorting in torment.

There was a loud, squishy popping noise, and the Orwell Disk plopped from Roger's forehead into Blade's left palm. A trickle of blood seeped from the circular identation left in Roger's forehead.

"Did you remove the damn thing?" Roger asked hopefully.

Blade held the disk out for Roger to see.

Hickok uttered a derisive snort. "If the blamed things are that easy to pry off, why didn't you take it off yourself?"

"The penalty for removing an O.D. is death," Roger replied.

Blade handed the Orwell Disk to the gunman. "You know what to do with it."

Hickok nodded. Seconds later, the disk was sailing out a narrow opening in the cargo door.

"I'm in your debt for this," Roger said to Blade. "I'll do my best to get us out of here."

"First things first," Blade remarked.

"What do you mean?"

Blade peered out the canopy at the buildings zipping past. "Where would the Superiors take a mutant to be neutered?"

# 18

"What do you want?" Lynx asked the Superior, doing his best to imitate the floor supervisor's voice. Tom had been the same size, but his voice had been slightly higher.

"I want to check on your new arrival," the Superior said.

"New arrival?" Lynx repeated, wondering if the android meant him.

"His name is Lynx," the Superior stated. "We brought him over early this morning, before you arrived. I dropped his dossier on your desk, on your Incoming tray. But with all the paperwork on your desk, I was concerned you might not see it."

"I saw it," Lynx lied.

"This one is a troublemaker," the Superior mentioned. "If you require guards, I will have a detail posted."

Lynx nodded toward his former room. "We won't need guards. He's locked up safe and sound."

The Superior stared at the door to the room. "I'd like to see him."

"You can't!" Lynx blurted out.

Melody anxiously licked her lips.

The Superior studied the feline mutant. "Why can't I see Lynx, Tom?"

"Because . . ." Lynx responded hastily. "He did give us some trouble when we tried to feed him, and he had to be sedated. He'll be out for four, maybe six hours."

The Superior nodded knowingly. "I knew he would be a problem. I will order a guard detail posted, and no one will be permitted in the room other than yourself and Melody."

Lynx nodded enthusiastically. "That's an excellent idea, now that I think of it. Don't let anybody in his room. He's too dangerous at that."

"Report to me if he creates another disturbance," the Superior ordered.

"Without delay," Lynx responded.

The Superior wheeled and walked away.

Lynx headed for the stairwell, Melody on his right side. "Who the hell was that?" he whispered.

"WW-60," Melody answered. "He handles administrative coordination for this section."

"Do you think we fooled him?" Lynx queried.

"If we hadn't," Melody replied, "we'd be in custody right now."

They walked to the stairwell door, deliberately conveying a casual air, but once in the stairwell they increased their pace, speeding up the steps as rapidly as their legs would carry them. They reached the door to Floor 45 without mishap.

Lynx hesitated, his left hand on the knob. "How do we play this? Won't we be suspicious if we march on in and ask to see my buddies?"

Melody reflected for a minute. "What are their names?"

"Gremlin and Ferret," Lynx said.

"I have an idea," Melody stated. "Follow my lead."

Lynx opened the door, then unexpectedly halted.

A Superior was standing not six feet away, leafing through a handful of papers. He looked up and saw them. "Hello. May I assist you?"

Melody moved past Lynx, smiling sweetly. "Sorry to bother you, but I believe you have two new arrivals here for testing. Their names are Gremlin and Ferret."

The android nodded. "They're in 45-C taking the written portion of the Psychological Profile Examination."

"The Examination will need to be interrupted," Melody said.

The Superior lowered the papers. "Why?"

"We've subjected their companion, the one called Lynx, to a routine medical exam," Melody said. "WW-60 sent us up as soon as he saw the results."

"What results?"

Melody feigned abject dismay. "We were appalled to discover Lynx has a communicable sexual disease. Syphilis."

"Sexually transmitted diseases were eliminated from our stock decades ago," the Superior commented.

"From *our* stock, yes," Melody agreed. "But these mutants are from outside Androxia, correct?"

"What does WW-60 require?" the Superior asked.

"He wants Gremlin and Ferret tested right away," Melody said. "We can't have these degenerates mingling with our pure stock if they're infected. WW-60 is preparing the proper papers, but those forms take a while to complete. He wanted to know if you would send Gremlin and Ferret down with us, and he assures you the release forms will be on your desk within the hour."

"A reasonable request," the Superior stated. "Wait here. I will bring them out." He turned and moved down the corridor.

Lynx nudged Melody's left elbow. "Syphilis?"

"It was the best I could do on the spur of the moment," Melody said.

Lynx smiled. "I'm shocked, princess. A lady like you, comin' up with a disease like that!" He laughed.

"It was the first thing I thought of when you kissed me," Melody explained.

Lynx's eyebrows tried to leave his face. "But *you* kissed *me*!"

Melody grinned mischievously. "I must be a gambler at heart."

"I don't have no sexual diseases!" Lynx snapped, miffed. "I'm as healthy as they come."

"I'll bet," Melody said, chuckling.

The Superior emerged from one of the rooms with two mutants in tow.

"That's them," Lynx verified in a hushed tone.

Gremlin, walking behind the Superior, spotted Lynx and opened his mouth to yell a greeting. Before he could, however, Ferret reached up and clamped his right hand over Gremlin's mouth. The Superior never noticed.

"I can see you're the brains of the bunch," Melody said softly.

Lynx puffed up his chest. "As a matter of fact, I am."

"No wonder you're all prisoners," Melody whispered, and then the Superior was within hearing range.

"Here they are," the android said. "Do you want me to accompany you?"

"Thank you, but that won't be necessary," Melody told him.

"They might attempt to escape," the Superior observed.

"We'll take the evevator then," Melody proposed. "They can't escape from an elevator."

"A logical alternative," the Superior concurred, and turned. "Follow me," he directed Gremlin and Ferret.

Lynx and Melody brought up the rear as they walked down the corridor until they reached the elevator.

"I will be expecting the release forms as promised," the Superior said to Melody.

"WW-60 will see they reach you," Melody affirmed. She pressed the button for the elevator.

Lynx stepped up to Gremlin and Ferret. "You two will behave or suffer the consequences."

"Whatever you say, sir," Ferret said meekly.

"That's the right attitude," Lynx stated imperiously.

"We've learned our lesson," Ferret went on. "We don't want any trouble. We never did. It was our friend Lynx who gave you Androxians such a hard time. He's always getting us into hot water. I guess he can't help himself."

"What?" Lynx stated.

"That's right, sir," Ferret continued. "Lynx combines monumental stupidity with a supreme arrogance. He blunders his way through life, creating more problems than he's worth."

"That's enough about this Lynx," Lynx said.

"Yes, sir." Ferret then ignored him. "Lynx is about the dumbest nincompoop this side of the Milky Way. I've heard you perform lobotomies here, and you would be doing the world a favor if you performed one on Lynx. Of course, you probably won't find anything in his head worth lobotomizing—"

"That's enough!" Lynx declared angrily.

"Yes, sir," Ferret said in a suddued fashion.

The elevator arrived with a clang, the door sliding open.

Lynx motioned for Ferret and Gremlin to enter.

"Thank you," Melody addressed the android. "We'll contact you as soon as the test results are known."

Lynx stepped into the elevator.

"All mutants should be as efficient as you," the Superior complimented Melody.

Melody smiled and joined the others. Her right hand reached up, and she tapped one of the buttons on the control panel to the right of the door.

The elevator door closed.

Melody pressed the button for the ground floor.

"Lynx!" Ferret exclaimed in delight. "How did you do it?"

Lynx gave Ferret an icy stare. "It was easy, even for a nincompoop like me."

"Some people can't take a joke," Ferret retorted.

Lynx glanced at Gremlin, who was gawking at Melody. "And what's with you, birdbrain? Why are you so quiet?"

"Where did you find such a lovely woman, yes?" Gremlin asked.

Melody grinned. "I take back what I said, Lynx. You're not the brains of the bunch."

Lynx introduced his friends, pointing at each one in turn. "Ferret and Gremlin, I'd like you to meet Melody. She's my squeeze."

"I'm your *what*?" Melody queried. She looked up at the floor indicator lights above the door.

Ferret executed an elaborate bow. "My pleasure, dear lady! Seldom have I encountered a woman of such exquisite beauty. I expect you are endowed with an intelligence the equal of your loveliness, although your taste in men leaves me in doubt."

"Why you—!" Lynx said, bristling.

"Quiet!" Melody commanded. "We don't have much time. The elevator will be on the ground floor soon. This particular elevator shaft is located at the rear of the reception area. With any luck, we won't bump into any Superiors. When it stops and the doors open, take a right. There's an exit door to the rear parking lot about ten feet from this elevator. Ferret and Gremlin, keep your heads down or turn them to the rear wall. We don't want anyone in the reception area to notice you're not wearing O.D.'s."

Gremlin indicated the gleaming disk on Lynx's forehead. "Is that for real, yes?"

"No," Lynx responded. "It's a fake. I'm rippin' the sucker off as soon as we're out of here."

"Too bad," Ferret said. "You'll have problems with the draft again."

"Draft?" Lynx repeated, puzzled. "What draft?"

"The draft from the hole in your head the disk is covering," Ferret stated, and cackled.

Lynx looked at Melody and sighed. "With friends like these two clowns, you can see why the last thing I need is more enemies."

The elevator came to an abrupt stop and the door opened.

The reception area was spacious. Chairs lined the green walls and were organized in rows across the red carpet. A large circular wooden counter was positioned near the front door, staffed by three women in white uniforms and a Superior. Neither the android, the women, nor any of the humans and mutants seated in the chairs paid the scantest attention to the elevator's arrival.

"Hurry!" Melody urged, leading the way to the right, nervously scanning the reception area, dreading the outcome if they were detected and apprehended.

Lynx marched up to the exit door as if he didn't have a care in the world, reaching it a step behind Melody. He grabbed the knob, then glanced at Ferret and Gremlin. "I don't intend to get caught again. They're not takin' me alive this time! So once we're out this door, we do whatever it takes to stay free. I don't care if there's a hundred Superiors waitin' for us out there." He paused. "And if something should happen to me, I want you two bozos to make sure Melody reaches the Home. Got it?"

Gremlin and Ferret nodded.

Lynx squared his shoulders and twisted the doorknob, then shoved, prepared to sell his life dearly, if necessary, to safeguard Melody.

But there weren't one hundred Superiors waiting for them.

There wasn't a Superior anywhere in sight.

There were dozens of vehicles, and a number of mutants and humans moving from the parking lot to the Medical Building or going the other way.

Lynx moved outside. He saw an entranceway 30 yards to the right. Then he looked to the left.

Fifty yards distant, resting on a concrete helipad, was a sleek white helicopter.

"Do you see what I see?" Lynx asked.

"I see it," Ferret confirmed.

"If the pilot is still on board," Lynx said, "we'll have our ticket out of here."

They hurried toward the helipad.

Melody repeatedly glanced at the parking lot, hoping no one

would become unduly curious if they beheld two mutants in loincloths hastening from the Medical Building. She breathed an audible sigh of relief when they reached the edge of the helipad, and she eagerly scrambled over the top after the others. A startling thought slowed her down, though, as she stood on the concrete: if Lynx, Ferret, and Gremlin all wore those deplorable loincloths, was it possible all mutants, even the women, wore them where Lynx was from? She saw Lynx approaching an open sliding door on the side of the chopper, and she opened her mouth to question him.

Lynx was just about to climb onto the copter when a glimmering pair of revolver barrels poked around the right edge of the door. He leaped back, crouching, his claws extended, snarling in fury at being thwarted when they were so close to freedom. So close!

That was when a grinning blond man in buckskins appeared in the doorway, a revolver in each hand. "Howdy, runt," he said to Lynx. "What's the matter with you? Have you got ants in your britches?"

Melody would never forget Lynx's response. She'd failed to recognize, until that very moment, exactly how many curse words there were in the English langauge.

# 19

Two months later the Family celebrated the arrival of their missing members with the biggest bash ever held at the Home. After imbibing enough wine to drown a horse, Sherry publicly declared she was chaining Hickok to their bed and not letting him go for a week. She did not live up to her word, however, as the gunman was seen three days later walking rather stiffly around the compound.

Melody and Roger were formally accepted into the Family. After Melody recited her pledge of Loyalty, the Family women collectively presented her with a welcoming gift consisting of three hand-sewn outfits. No one could quite understand her reaction, though, when she actually hugged the clothing and kept saying, over and over again, "Thank you! Thank you!"

One month after their return, Blade and Hickok officiated at the induction of three new Warriors and the creation of a new Triad. Bravo Triad was formed, and its member Warriors were the only three male mutants in the Family. Lynx was ecstatic, Gremlin expressed genuine happiness, but Ferret was oddly reserved. Later that night, while Blade was patrolling the east wall, he saw Ferret standing by himself in a secluded section of the Home and gazing up at the stars. He distinctly overheard Ferret ask aloud: "Why me?"

# AFTER THE NUCLEAR WAR WAS OVER—THE REAL KILLING BEGAN

They called him Phoenix because he rose from the ashes of destruction, driven by hatred, and thirsting for revenge. Battling nature gone insane and men driven mad by total devastation, he forged his way across a nightmare landscape.

The action/adventure series that's hotter than a thermonuclear explosion, by

## DAVID ALEXANDER

_____2462-4  #1:  DARK MESSIAH
$2.95 US/$3.75 CAN

_____2517-5  #2:  GROUND ZERO
$2.95 US/$3.75 CAN

_____2571-X  #3:  DEATH QUEST
$2.95US/$3.75 CAN